YESTERDAY'S DREAM

D1652065

YO - EGz - 430

YESTERDAY'S DREAM

•

JoAnn Sands

AVALON BOOKS
NEW YORK

© Copyright 1999 by JoAnn Sands
Library of Congress Catalog Card Number: 99-90719
ISBN 0-8034-9376-2
All rights reserved.
All the characters in this book are fictitious,
and any resemblance to actual persons,
living or dead, is purely coincidental.
Published by Thomas Bouregy & Co., Inc.
401 Lafayette Street, New York, NY 10003

PRINTED IN THE UNITED STATES OF AMERICA
ON ACID-FREE PAPER
BY HADDON CRAFTSMEN, BLOOMSBURG, PENNSYLVANIA

To my "church family" at Colebrookdale Chapel

Chapter One

"Better not do it; it's too risky. . . . But then suppose it were me?" Abigail Kenan argued with herself aloud as she viewed the girl up ahead, thumbing a ride in the chilly Saturday afternoon drizzle. Applying the brake of her rented car cautiously, she swung out around her, careful not to splash her. The girl certainly wasn't dressed for the weather. Though she was wearing low boots, she wore no coat. Her bulky sweater clung to her thin form.

Abbie glanced in her rearview mirror, noticing the hitch-hiker's shoulders slump as she once again continued to walk along the winding country road. Rolling her eyes, Abbie gave in to her soft heart, knowing Jamie would scold if he knew she even contemplated the idea of picking up a stranger. Yet she knew if he were now driving, he would do the same, for she'd been seated beside him in his old Jeep when he'd done just that. He'd grinned bashfully and said, "If it were me, I'd want a lift. Besides, he looks safe enough." She knew he had a pistol beneath his safari coat to protect them from a charging animal or dangerous snake, although she never knew him to think of using it on a human being. He relied on his communications skills for that, and Jamie was a gifted communicator.

1

Abigail stopped, put the car in reverse, and backed up. The girl began to run toward her before she could change her mind, yanked the door open, and shimmied in. Abbie's initial thought was that she had made a mistake. The hitchhiker's eyes were heavily made up with black mascara and eye-liner, which was smeared down a cheek bearing a star tattoo. She appeared to be about sixteen, but then it was hard to tell because of all the makeup. Her blond hair had been piled up in a "punk" style of sorts but the nasty weather had ruined the effect she'd wanted. A visible shiver ran through the girl's body.

"Not the best of days to be out walking, is it," Abbie commented as she shifted her foot from the brake to the accelerator. Then, reaching over, she eased the heater fan on a degree warmer. "There, you'll soon be more comfortable. Where are you heading?"

"Laurel Springs."

"Then you're in luck; that's my destination too. This would have been a long, cold walk for you. We're about fifty miles north."

"I know."

Abigail glanced over at her once again. She sat up straight and tense and fidgeted with hands that did not carry a purse. . . . hands that rested on conspicuously bare knees. She wore a black miniskirt and no jewelry except for a thin gold chain bearing a cross which hung from her neck. She didn't appear to be dressed for a trip to Laurel Springs. Could she be a runaway? Abigail wondered as she tried to strike up a conversation. "It's rather dangerous these days for a young woman to be hitchhiking, don't you think?"

The girl stared straight ahead, through the gentle swipe of the wipers as they momentarily cleared the path of vision before the heavy mist blurred it again. "I reckon," she said in a distinct Southern drawl, "it's as dangerous for you to

Yesterday's Dream

take a chance on me as it is for me to take a chance on you. Do you make a habit of picking up hitchhikers?''

''No. Do you make it a habit of being picked up?''

''No, ma'am. Not unless I got no choice.'' She leaned closer to the vent to feel the welcomed heat, then lifted her arm and wiped her cheek with her sweater sleeve. Abbie was glad to see the tattoo wasn't real. It smeared.

It would be a shame to disfigure what could be a pretty face, she thought, then asked, ''What's your name?''

The girl paused so long that Abigail was sure she wasn't going to answer, but finally she said, ''Tricia,'' through tight lips.

''Tricia what?''

''Just Tricia. Look, I don't mean to be rude, but I'd rather not talk the miles away, if you don't mind.''

''All right, Just Tricia, whatever you want.''

A quiet *humph!* was her reply. Abbie stole a sideways glance and thought something looked vaguely familiar about this girl. Just what, she didn't know, only that there was. . . . And she was more certain than ever that Tricia was running from something. She wished she would confide in her. She had a heart to help if she could. The girl had purposely avoided making eye contact with Abbie, throwing up a wall that couldn't be bridged without invitation, regardless of the fact that she was sitting as an invited passenger in Abbie's car.

Abigail honored her request by not talking, but it was hard. She was returning home after a six-year absence, and she knew she was coming back to a life that would never be quite the same. Knowing neither of the men in her life would be there left her with a hollow feeling inside. But she mustn't think about that now lest a tear escape, and Abbie was no more anxious to speak to her past than this teenager was. I was about her age when my heart was broken, she thought.

4   *JoAnn Sands*

Abbie gripped the wheel and shifted in her seat. Had the small town changed much? Probably not. Considering where she'd been, Laurel Springs would seem like a cozy paradise.

"Have you been to the Springs before?" Abbie asked, breaking the silence she was determined to speak anyway.

Tricia bobbed her head mutely.

"Other than a brief weekend funeral, I haven't been back in a half dozen years."

"It hasn't changed," Tricia verified. "Nothing ever changes," she mumbled, and Abbie thought her statement held a deep and personal hurt.

By now the drizzle had turned into a steady rain. Up ahead, Abbie caught sight of the flashing neon lights of the Mountain View Cafe. Slowing down, she flipped on her blinker and turned into the gravel lot, parking next to a utility truck. Near the entrance was a sandwich board bearing the picture of a shapely blonde in a fringed cowgirl outfit. Below were the words, "Country Western Night Presents Miss Becki Bartlett. Wednesday and Friday Nights."

Bare bones advertising for a country singing star wannabe, Abbie thought with a languid smile. She'd known that feeling too—seemingly a lifetime ago.

"What are you doing?" Tricia asked, breaking into Abigail's thoughts.

"It's foolish to drive around these mountain roads in such weather. Visibility's lousy, but I don't think it'll last. We'll wait it out inside. Hopefully a breeze will push the fog away."

"You don't think we'll get a . . ." the girl broke off, biting her lip, and looked away.

"A what?" Abbie prodded, but it was obvious Tricia didn't want to talk about what "it" was. Changing the

Yesterday's Dream

subject, she forced cheerfulness into her voice. "I'm just dying for a hamburger!"

"You'll be sorry. I hear they're known for their grease."

"Fine. Then I'll order some soup." Turning off the ignition, she reached on the floor for her umbrella. "If we hurry, maybe we won't get too wet."

"In case you haven't noticed, I already am." She hugged her arms around her waist and leaned slightly forward toward the vent which was no longer comforting her with its heat. "I'll wait for you while you eat."

"Oh, no you won't. Something tells me if I let you alone in this vehicle, you'll be gone by the time I come out."

"You'd care?"

"Yes. Don't ask me why, but I would. Maybe it's your congenial personality."

Tricia looked at her and their eyes held for the first time. The vaguest of smiles touched the girl's lips. "I think you mean that."

"I do. Come on, let's go."

The teenager got out reluctantly. With one hand holding the large umbrella over them, Abbie slid her arm around the girl's waist as they hurried toward the double glass doors. She glanced at the sandwich board as they passed. With hair and a figure like that, this singer just might make it. Abbie knew, if Becki had a good voice, she'd be competition on the local circuit. A smile touched her lips. She'd never really taken any serious first step toward her "youthful dreams," Abbie thought as they stepped inside.

Abbie led the way over to one of the eight square tables. A trucker sat at the counter talking to a young waitress. It took the waitress a few moments to tear herself away from his company to bring them the menu, which she plopped drown unceremoniously.

"Order whatever looks good to you, Tricia."

When the waitress returned with her pad a few minutes

6   *JoAnn Sands*

later, Abbie decided on a bowl of vegetable soup. "Tricia?" she invited.

The girl lifted an unsure brow. "Your treat?"

"Yes."

"In that case, I'll have a hamburger with the works."

Now Abbie arched her brow. "I thought you said they were greasy."

She shrugged her shoulders. "I don't know, it's just what I heard."

Abbie looked up at the waitress, who looked anxious to get back to the company of the truck driver. "Bring a bowl of vegetable soup for my friend too. It'll warm her up."

As soon as she left, Tricia leaned forward, the heels of her hands on the edge of the table. "Why are you doing this? I don't have any money."

"I thought I already told you, it's my treat."

"But why? I don't understand. Strangers generally don't do random acts of kindness for each other. What do you get out of it anyway?"

"The satisfaction of seeing you get a decent meal. Bet it's been a while, hasn't it?"

Tricia ignored the question but looked at her suspiciously.

"People don't give someone anything unless they want something in return. So, what is it you want?"

"Some civility would be nice." Abbie reached for her glass of water and sipped it. "I'll never take this for granted again. We don't really appreciate things until suddenly, we find ourselves outside our comfort zone and without them. Where are you coming from, Tricia? Geographically speaking," she asked, practically in the same breath.

"New York," she surprised her by answering. "I took a bus down to Asheville and waited a half hour for my transfer. Meanwhile, someone stole my suitcase and pocketbook which held my ticket and money."

Yesterday's Dream   7

"I'm sorry."

She shrugged. "It's life . . . it happens." She smiled shyly and found herself genuinely curious. "Where are you coming from?"

"Brazil."

Her eyes widened. "As in South America?"

"That's right."

"Wow! What were you doing there?"

For the first time, Abbie noticed real interest behind her question. "During the past two years, I've been teaching in a mission school."

"You're a missionary?"

"Not exactly. I just teach Brazilian children the three Rs."

"Oh? Well . . . I didn't think you were a real one—missionary, I mean."

Abbie grinned, playing along with her. "Why not?"

"Well . . ." she said again, reaching for a logical explanation, but she knew as soon as the words left her mouth, it wasn't. "You don't look like one."

"And what is a missionary supposed to look like?"

Tricia's eyes wandered over Abbie's pretty face, her pixie-cut auburn hair, and twinkling green eyes. At last she shrugged. "I don't know. You're too young for one thing. I guess I always pictured them as spinster-types, wearing wire-frame glasses and homemade dresses and with graying hair secured back in a bun."

Now Abbie tossed back her head and laughed outright, catching the fleeting attention of the waitress and the trucker. "You have the single part right, though I'm scarcely a spinster at twenty-three."

Tricia didn't join in in her laughter. "There's something about you. . . ." Her voice trailed off as she shook her head, unsure. "I think it's your laugh. I feel I should know you from somewhere."

Abbie sobered as she surveyed the teen's face. "You know, I've had the same feeling about you." But she couldn't explore the common feeling deeper, for at that point the waitress brought them their food.

Abigail thought Tricia ate as though she hadn't in days. She gobbled her soup and hamburger almost simultaneously and stopped short of licking the bowl clean. Wiping her mouth with a paper napkin, she looked at Abbie almost timidly. "Thanks, Miss . . . oh, golly . . . what did you say your name was?"

"I don't believe I did. It's Abigail—Abigail Kenan—but folks around here have called me Abbie since I can remember."

Recognition and displeasure flickered in Tricia's eyes. "Why didn't you tell me who you were?"

"You didn't ask. I wanted to introduce myself but you didn't want to talk, remember?"

"You still should have told me."

"You know now. But I still don't know your last name. Or is that some big secret?"

"It's Rossi."

Now it was Abbie's turn for her eyes to widen and her lips to form an O in surprise. She snapped her fingers. "Of course. Patti Rossi."

"So, you remember me too. But I don't go by Patti anymore. It sounds so juvenile."

The barrier that Abbie had slowly dismantled was going right back up again, and she couldn't understand why. She remembered Patti Rossi all right. She was the precocious eleven-year-old who made her presence known at the most inopportune times. And that brought "him" to mind, not that he was ever very far from her memory.

"How is David?" she asked in a voice that she hoped sounded casual, but the teen seemed too preoccupied with herself to notice the hurt in Abbie's tone.

Yesterday's Dream   9

"How should I know? I've been away for a year and he's been gone for a lot more."

"I thought maybe you kept in touch."

"David's not much of a letter writer."

"I know." She rose slowly. "Excuse me for a few minutes while I freshen up. I won't be long."

As Abigail stared at her reflection in the smudged restroom mirror a few moments later, she wasn't surprised that neither had recognized the other. The last time Patti had seen her, Abbie's long hair was parted in the center and she wore braces and wire-frame glasses. She wasn't dressed in her former sweatshirt and jeans either, but a stunning jade pantsuit with gold accessories. "Green is your color, lass," Jamie told her whenever he saw her wearing it. She fingered her oval locket, a gift from David on her sixteenth birthday. It had contained the pictures of the two men most dear to her—her father and David—until her friendship with Jamie became serious. When the charismatic Scotsman proposed to her three months ago, she accepted. "I've got no ring to give you now, Abigail, but I will see that you have the finest just as soon as I'm able. That's a promise."

And he would, knowing Jamie MacIlhaney as she did. He was a man of honor, a man her father would approve of. A man who would be coming soon to Laurel Springs to claim her as his bride.

Abigail applied a fresh coat of mauve lipstick and a matching blush to her cheeks, then ran a comb through her short hair and finally separated her bangs. Her lashes needed no mascara, for she was generously blessed with thick lashes like her mother. People told her she also had inherited her mother's infectious laugh, but with her father's strong stubborn will and feel for justice even when she had to stand alone. It took a measure of strength and determination to live as she had the past two years. Now she was looking forward to resting at her mother's estate and yes, perhaps being pampered a little bit before she began a brand-new phase of her life as a missionary doctor's wife.

Zipping her shoulder bag closed, Abbie walked from the small, paint-peeling restroom to the table where she'd left Patti. She was gone!

Abbie glanced about the room. So was the trucker. If she hitched a ride into town with that guy . . . she thought, with a sigh of dismay. However, when Abbie stepped outside, she saw the trucker had left and Tricia was sitting stoically on the front seat of her red car. She walked quickly, avoiding the mud puddles in the pot-holed lot. It had stopped raining now, but the skies were still a smudged gray while the smokelike swirls of fog moved almost gracefully along the pine-covered hill nearby. Shaking the remaining drops off her folded umbrella, she opened the back door and tossed it on the seat with her rugged canvas bags.

"You gave me a start. For a moment there, I thought you took off with the trucker."

"I might be a little desperate, but I'm not stupid."

After buckling up, Abbie backed around and pulled out onto the sparsely traveled road. "Do your parents know you're coming home?"

There was mild surprise on Tricia's face when she looked at Abbie's profile. "Don't you know?"

"Know what?"

"That Sheila left Daddy a year and a half ago."

"Oh, Patti," she sighed, forgetting to use her requested name. "I'm sorry to hear it finally came to that." There had been talk—there was always talk about high-profile people in the community, and the Rossis had been fair game. She was more than a little curious why Sheila left

Yesterday's Dream

her family but didn't ask. Instead, she asked, "Does your dad know you're coming?"

"Yeah, he knows." Her lack of enthusiasm spoke volumes. "Sheila was more than thrilled to provide me with the bus fare to return. It didn't work out; whatever made me think it would." She paused a moment, then admitted, "I'm glad you came along when you did and were willing to pick up a stranger."

"Who, as it turned out, wasn't."

"Yeah. My feet were killing me, I was cold and hungry. I don't think I could have walked fifty miles and I sure wasn't about to call Daddy to come and pick me up."

"He would have, knowing your father."

"Sure he would have, after he reminded me I was still the same irresponsible kid that I was a year ago. I don't need that." She heaved a tired sigh, then leaned forward, her mood vacillating between hope and despair. Now it was on the swing back up. "I wonder if there will be banners or ribbons?"

"What?" Abbie queried, not sure what the teen was referring to.

"Ribbons. You know, like in that old song, 'Tie A Yellow Ribbon.' I wonder if Daddy will have ribbons welcoming me home."

"We'll soon find out," Abbie said, coming off the mountain road and entering the town of Laurel Springs. It wasn't a prosperous community, as there were no big industries—just a furniture factory that had seen better times and a few "Mom & Pop" businesses. Abbie's great-great-grandfather had founded the town after the Civil War and named it Laurel, after his wife, and Springs because of the abundant amount of water that bubbled up from the foothills.

As they came down the long hill, a tall white steeple could be seen spiraling up through a maze of pines. Tricia leaned forward, her hand on the dash, her anxious eyes fixed on the building. Then a smile cracked her tense face. ''I see some sort of banner draped across the pillars.''

''It must be your 'welcome home' banner, Tricia.''

''Then Daddy has forgiven me. You can't imagine how worried I've been, not knowing. On the phone he sounded so . . .'' Her sentence died on her lips, and she slumped back, dejected. Abbie read the words. It was a welcome home banner all right, but it didn't spell out Tricia's name.

Normally it would have thrilled Abbie, knowing her name was up there for all who drove by the little country church to see. But not today—not with the Reverend's hurting daughter sitting next to her. ''Tricia, I'm sorry. But don't read more into this than you should. It doesn't mean he's not glad you're coming home.''

The girl shrugged. ''It's no big deal. After all, it's you who deserves to come back to a heroine's welcome. Not me. I've just been another embarrassment.''

Abbie didn't know what to say, so she didn't say anything, knowing no matter how well-meaning her words, they would fall short of the mark. A couple minutes later, she braked to a stop in front of the one-story parsonage.

''Would you like me to go in with you?''

''No.'' Though there was a hint of uncertainty in her tone, Tricia lifted her chin in determination. She was an almost adult and she didn't need the help of this woman. She was in the process of reaching for the door when Abbie caught her lightly by the wrist.

''Wait a moment.'' Then, taking a tissue from her purse, she wiped away at Tricia's cheek. ''I have a feeling your dad isn't into tattoos, either permanent or temporary.'' She drew back to survey her. ''There, that's better.'' But still maybe not acceptable. Abbie knew Bill Rossi wouldn't be pleased with all her heavy eye makeup and choice of clothing. She could only hope he wouldn't be too critical.

Yesterday's Dream　　　　13

Tricia opened the door and slid out, then ducked her head to look in the window at Abbie. ''Thanks for the soup and burger.''

''You're welcome. If you want to call or see me sometime, I'll be staying at my mother's for a few weeks. You know where she lives.''

''Yeah. That white mansion on the knoll. See you around. 'Bye.'' And with that said, Tricia turned and walked, with her head down, toward the small brown-frame parsonage. Abbie watched from the side of the road, chewing her lip fretfully and hoping that when she got to the door, Reverend Rossi would be there to gather her in his arms and dispel her uncertainties. But it appeared there was no one there to greet her at least no one visible. The door opened and closed, shutting Tricia from her view.

''Ah, lass,'' she could almost hear Jamie say now as he had on so many occasions. ''You're so much like that Abigail of old, trying to be peace-maker. You've got to stop feeling you must nurture every hurtin' creature, 'cause you can't do it. And tryin' will only get you into trouble someday.''

Jamie was right, Abbie thought, as she pulled away from the curb. But Patti was special and she'd give a lot to help her and bring peace to her family.

Chapter Two

Chestnut Hill was exactly as Abbie last saw it, and pretty much as the white Greek Revival dwelling looked when it was built about one hundred and thirty years ago. She had hardly gotten out of the car when Margaret Kenan came rushing out of the house into the light drizzle, her arms outstretched to embrace her daughter.

"Oh honey, it's about time. I've been looking for you for hours. With the weather being so damp and dreary, I was afraid . . . well, never mind. I'm just glad you're finally home."

"Me too, Mom. It's too wet to be standing outside without your jacket on. Let's go inside before you catch your death of a cold." Interlocking arms, they began to walk up the wide steps onto the pillar-supported porch.

"I still think you should have let me meet you at the airport," Maggie chided as she opened the door.

Ruby Brown, who had refrained from rushing outside but nonetheless looked just as jubilant, now spoke up. "It's a good thing she didn't. Your mama was called out before dawn to deliver the Hopkins baby, and she didn't get back till noon. She would have left you stranded at the airport.

14

Yesterday's Dream 15

The good Lord knew she needed something else to occupy her mind other than your homecomin'," Ruby finished with a hefty laugh as she gathered Abbie in her arms for a smothering hug.

Ruby had been with the Kenan family ever since Abigail was born. Though she was a hired nanny, the family liked her so well that when she was no longer needed, they offered her the position of housekeeper, and Ruby, who enjoyed working for the Kenans, was quick to take it. Twenty-three years later, she was more than an employee. She was a trusted and dear friend.

Ruby took her coat and hung it up in the closet. "Looks to me like you've been livin' too long on them rice and beans. You've lost weight. Give me a little time, I'll fill out our girl with my fried chicken and sweet potato pie," she finished, winking behind her silver wire-frame glasses at Maggie.

Abbie tossed back her head and laughed, not offended by Ruby's statement. "I'm looking forward to your pampering already."

"I wasn't quite sure when to expect you, so I made plenty, thinkin' I could heat some up later in the microwave oven if needed. But you're here now, so you and your mama can eat together. You must be hungry."

Abbie didn't have the heart to tell her that soup at the Mountain View Cafe had satisfied her appetite. Instead, she turned to her mother whose proud eyes hadn't left her face for an instant. "I'm glad I arrived before you ate, but do you mind if I call Jamie first and let him know I've arrived safely?"

"Go right ahead, honey. While you're doing that, Ruby and I will get your things from your car and take them to your room."

Sliding her hand along the oak railing, Abbie ascended the spiral staircase and walked down the hall to her father's

16 *JoAnn Sands*

den. There had been no changes made since he passed away three years ago. It was as though it had become a memorial to a man her mother obviously found it difficult to let go of. A family portrait, the last one taken before Abigail went off to college, was on the desk—mother, father and daughter smiling happily in their Sunday clothes to be recorded in the church directory. It was the first time Laurel Springs Chapel had had a photo directory, and she was glad now that her father wanted to be included, for this was the last portrait taken before his untimely death at age fifty-nine.

Abbie sank down in his massive, brass-studded leather swivel chair. What a contrast to Jamie's folding metal one which he used at his battered desk in the jungle.

"It'll do for now, Abbie," he'd tell her. "Someday, things will be different when I have my own practice." She knew her father would be appalled by the primitiveness of his practice in a country where nearly half the population was under fifteen. But what Jamie lacked in technology, he more than made up for in a generous and caring heart for the very people to whom his own father had been a missionary doctor a generation before. Though born and raised in the Amazon Basin, he had been educated in Edinburgh only to return one day to take over for his ailing parent. He'd been working in that capacity for the past six years.

Reaching for the phone, Abbie touched a series of buttons and in a short while was speaking to Jamie. He was relieved to know she'd arrived safely, but his tone lacked his usual energy, and his voice sounded tired. He explained he'd had a busy day which began at four-thirty when someone was brought to the clinic with a ruptured appendix. This was the first time he'd had a chance to sit down and grab a bite to eat.

"What are you eating?" she asked, hearing the clinking of metal.

"Salmon. Great source of calcium."

Yesterday's Dream

"Your days of eating your meals out of a can are numbered, Jamie," she teased. "On the plus side, keeping busy you don't have the time to miss me."

"Wrong. I miss not having supper with you right now, and I'll miss not having our evening strolls and quiet conversation later. It's full moon tonight, lass. Look up and think about me knowing I'll be thinking of you."

"It's been a rainy day here in the Carolinas, so there will be no visible moon, but I'll think about you when I snuggle down under the covers for the night." She wound the cord about her finger. "I'm calling from Daddy's study. There's some things here I want to give you, if it's okay with Mom."

"I hope you've found her well."

"Yes. She's keeping busy being visiting nurse and midwife to the community. Since Dad passed away, it's left us with no doctor in Laurel Springs. I bet when you see this place, you'll want to remedy that."

"Right now the only thing I want from your community is you."

They talked several minutes longer. She told him about her uneventful flight home, but neglected to mention she picked up a hitchhiker before knowing who she was. Perhaps if she had told him about the Rossis before, it would have been different. But she had never mentioned David and his kid sister. Then, with a promise of talking again tomorrow about the same time, they said their goodbyes and Abbie left. But she didn't go directly downstairs. She stopped in front of the only other closed door along the upstairs hall. Hesitantly, she reached out and turned the knob. It was unlocked. Abbie opened the door slowly . . . almost with dread . . . and gazed inside. Even though darkness was encroaching, she could make out its contents and her heart sank.

"Oh, Mom," she sighed, resting her shoulder against the

door jamb. She had hoped that after all this time, the situation had changed. It hadn't.

A few minutes later, Abbie found her mother in the large modern kitchen, helping Ruby put the finishing touches on supper. She'd decided not to say anything about ''the room,'' at least for now. Maggie smiled as she looked up from pouring the coffee into the china cups. She could pass for forty, Abbie thought. Her short blond hair was styled in an attractive cut, becoming her pretty face. Her blue eyes crinkled when she smiled, but other than that, there were no lines marking a life that had seen its share of happiness and heartbreak. Shadow, the black Lab Ruby had bought her the day after her father passed away, came into the kitchen, his nails clicking against the tile. He sniffed at her ankles, then lavished her with wet kisses of welcome.

Laughing, Abbie bent over and patted his head, while he looked up at her with big moist eyes. ''You've really gotten big since I've seen you last. You were just a pup then.''

''Shadow was a great source of comfort to me when I most needed it. Now he's part of the family.'' Maggie sat the pot back in its compartment under the cabinet. ''Could you reach Jamie?''

''Yes.'' She reached for a carrot stick and crunched into it. ''Poor man's had a hectic day. Says it's the first chance he's had to sit down or eat.''

Maggie *hummed* in agreement, having firsthand knowledge since she'd been married to a physician for nearly nineteen years. ''When did you say he'll be joining us?''

''In four or five days, just as soon as his replacement arrives.''

''That doesn't give me long to get this place in order.''

''Let me point out to you, Mom, it already is. There's nothing to be done, really. Jamie isn't used to elegance. His idea of gracious living is sleeping on a cot with clean sheets

Yesterday's Dream

and cooking off a generator-run hot plate. I'm afraid he'll find Chestnut Hill a bit overwhelming. I tried to describe it for him, but I got the impression he thought I was grossly exaggerating.''

Abbie went to the sink to wash her hands. Glancing over her shoulder, she continued. "As I told you, he has six weeks' leave before we have to go back to Brazil. He must fulfill his commitment to finish out another year there, then he'll be free to open his own practice here in the States. Hopefully then, he can slow down a bit and not feel so driven. He scarcely ever takes a day off.''

"I bet you don't either.''

"I teach at the mission school five days a week, Mom,'' Abbie reminded her, pulling out a chair to sit down.

"And the other two, you help doing what you can to make Jamie's burden a little lighter. I know you.'' Maggie draped her linen napkin over her lap. "And I'm so proud of you. The whole community is. But I must admit, when I heard those guerrillas took you and your students captive, I about had a coronary. I wished at that moment you were anywhere but down there in harm's way.''

"I can't afford to dwell on the what-might-have-beens. Thanks to Jamie, we were all released unharmed. He negotiated with them and thankfully they understood this was not the way to get things done.''

"I'm deeply indebted to him.''

"Me too.'' Abbie viewed the chicken, sweet potato pie, and corn and suddenly realized she was more hungry than she thought. "Everything looks so good. I can hardly wait for Jamie to enjoy this with me. Come on, let's eat!''

William Rossi looked at his quiet daughter from across the kitchen table. He wasn't sure how he felt—angry . . . relieved . . . joyful . . . sad—but he surmised it must be an amalgam of all these emotions. At that moment, though, he was feeling disappointment. Disappointment in a girl he felt had so much potential and in himself for somehow letting her down. That hurt.

Eight years ago well-meaning people told him he was taking a stranger into his home whose character had already been molded—that he was only setting himself up for heartache. He said they were wrong—that he and Sheila were just what Patti needed. Maybe. But as it turned out, Sheila didn't need them. That hurt too. It seemed most of his adult life consisted of a series of hurtful experiences.

Bill unconsciously raked his hand through his graying brown hair. He was a common-looking man with a somewhat hooked nose. When he smiled, his keen, deep-set eyes crinkled, and his cheeks went into grooves. Though not a particularly handsome face, it was one you could readily trust and warm to. He watched with a wrinkle on his heavy brow as Patti pushed the beans around on her paper plate. "I know hamburgers and baked beans aren't exactly a banquet," he spoke at last. "But all things considered, it's got to be better than some of the things you've had since you've run off."

"To set the record straight, Daddy, I didn't 'run off' and I haven't been picking through garbage cans for dinner. But I did have plenty of soup and sandwiches." She shrugged a bit helplessly. "Sheila's not the world's best cook."

He grunted in agreement, and she went on. "Actually, I'm still kind of full. I had a burger and a bowl of soup at the Mountain View Cafe."

"Thanks to Abigail," he said. From his vantage point behind the lace curtains, Bill had watched the teacher drop his daughter off. He'd wanted to gather Patti in his arms, to assure her the past was forgiven and they could begin anew. But he couldn't quite bring himself to do that. It was her idea to leave him and live in the big city with a woman who obviously didn't want her. Surely she knew that now.

Yesterday's Dream 21

If she'd shown any remorse for her past behavior and re-
belliousness and said, "Daddy, I'm sorry," he would have
forgiven her in an instant. Instead, he thought, she returns
with an arrogant air and that ridiculous makeup, which was
a negative statement in itself.

Bill took another bite from his rather dry burger, his gaze
on her face. Her eyes were downcast, staring at some in-
determinable spot on her plate. Those black eyelids annoyed him. "I understood you to say when you called me
that you were taking the bus home."

"That's right. But someone stole my pocketbook and
luggage on my layover."

"It's a good thing Abigail happened by or heaven knows
what might have happened to you."

"Would you have cared?" she challenged, looking up.
Their eyes met and held.

Bill shook his head sadly. "Ah, Patti, don't start in
already."

"Tricia."

"What?"

"Tricia," she repeated. "I call myself Tricia now. It
sounds more grown up."

"You think so?"

"I'm not the little naive girl you took in when my real
mom was killed in that tornado. Now—" she propped her
elbows up on the table and cupped her chin in her hands—
"what were you saying?"

"I was in the process of explaining to you that things
haven't been easy for me either. First the divorce, then a
runaway child. It's especially traumatic on a man who
holds my position. Right or wrong, we have to be an ex-
ample of a good and caring family to the people in this
community."

Tricia shrugged that bit of truth off. "At least you've
got a son who hasn't turned out so bad in spite of a some-

what bumpy start and . . .'' Patricia glanced around, and that's when it dawned on her that she hadn't seen her brother yet. Why not?

"I suppose," she said, answering her own question, though erroneously. "David's angry or ashamed of me too. But as I recall, he was no saint either when he was my age."

"No, he wasn't. But at least he returned to his senses." His mouth snapped shut. Heaven help him, he couldn't stop those words from slipping out.

She visibly stiffened. "And I haven't?"

"We'll see."

Tricia rose. "Look, if it's too much of a burden having me back in the house again, I'll leave."

"Sit down, Patti," Bill said in a no-nonsense tone, then waited a long moment for her to comply. He continued in a controlled timbre. "Contrary to what you may think, I am glad you're back, and you are welcome to stay for as long as you wish. However," he lifted an emphasizing finger, "while you're under my roof, you will listen to my house rules. You know very well what they are so I don't have to waste our time spelling them out."

"Yes, I know," she said with a bored roll of her eyes,

"Good. Now finish your supper and do the dishes. Then I want you to get changed. You can't go to the Community Hospital looking like that."

"I don't have anything else to wear. Someone stole my stuff, remember?"

"Yes, so you told me," Bill said, pressing his lips together. He remembered too that she had asked him to send all her clothing at home to her, and he did. "That outfit you're wearing . . . your mother approved of it? She let you run around New York looking like that?"

Tricia bristled. "I could have gone around naked for all she cared."

Yesterday's Dream   23

"Patricia!"

"And another thing, Sheila is not my mother. I must have been crazy to ever have thought she was."

Bill wiped a dab of mayonnaise from his lip. "I suppose we were both mistaken about that."

"Are you?" There was a longing in her tone, and he wasn't sure if he meant he was sorry that Sheila wasn't mother enough to take her off his hands or sorry that she'd been obviously so hurt by the woman she was reaching out to.

"Yes." He rose, wishing she would rise too. If she showed any desire for him to embrace her, he would, but he couldn't bear her rejection. "Tomorrow, after morning services, we'll go clothes shopping." Then he turned on his heel and started for the door.

As Tricia watched him leave, it struck her. "Daddy?" He turned expectantly and she went on. "Why must I go to the hospital?" she asked suspiciously, not knowing what lengths her father would go to satisfy himself that she really was okay.

At first Bill looked surprised at the question but he decided to answer honestly and ease her suspicion. "It's David," he was quick to assure her. "He had back surgery yesterday, but the doctor tells me he should be able to return home tomorrow. You couldn't have picked a better time to come back. David needs some care, and I sure could use the extra help around the house. And you need a place to stay while you contemplate what to do with the rest of your life. The way I see it, we all have something to gain here if we're willing to work through our problems."

For a long moment, David Rossi stared in dropped-jaw wonder at the skinny bare-legged kid in the black leather miniskirt. He began at her disheveled mop of blond hair and didn't stop until he reached her worn-heeled, low

24   *JoAnn Sands*

boots. Snapping his mouth shut, he said, "Patti?" unsure, as he tried to adjust himself into a more comfortable position. "Is that really you?"

Bill sucked in his breath, fully expecting Tricia to go on a tangent on how she no longer went by that juvenile-sounding name. Instead, she took an uncertain step forward, then her face broke into a smile for the first time. "In the flesh! How are you?" But the moment the question left her lips, she jumped in and answered it for him. "Obviously not very good or you wouldn't be here."

"Just for tonight, then ready or not, the hospital has to release me tomorrow."

She cast an unsure eye toward the silent, arm-folded man in the corner. "Daddy told me you had back surgery."

He nodded, his dark hair sliding over his forehead. "I fell."

"Playing softball with the little boys."

David grunted. "Anyway, they were hoping bed rest and therapy would do the trick, but no such luck. I reluctantly agreed to have the corrective surgery. I'll have to stay out of the classroom for a couple more weeks."

"So, who's in charge now?"

"Miss Larson."

"Lucille?" Tricia whistled, her eyes growing large. "Oh, wow! I thought she was put out to pasture years ago."

Bill spoke her name in disapproval. David, who found her outspokenness a little less offensive, smiled tolerantly. "She's a godsend, Patti. She came out of retirement and graciously postponed her plans for a trip to Florida. That is a true friend."

"Looks like things have a way of working out. You've got yourself a substitute teacher, and Daddy's volunteered me to be your nurse while you're convalescing."

Yesterday's Dream
25

"My nurse?" That wiped the easy smile off David's face. "What do you know about nursing?"

"Nothing," she admitted. "So maybe I can be your gofer."

"My gopher?"

"You know, someone who will run errands for you. Like bringing in the newspaper and mail. Make your lunch . . ."

"What do you know about cooking?" he dogged her with a teasing twinkle in his eyes.

The girl shrugged with an air of indifference. "What's so hard about shaking out a bowl of cornflakes or slapping some peanut butter and jelly sandwiches together?"

"Nothing, except I don't happen to like either."

"You'll get to." Tricia sank down on the edge of the bed and smiled almost shyly at her brother. She always liked David, and if there was one person on earth she ever looked up to, it was him. He was a gifted musician and vocalist, better she thought, than most. Tricia was so sure he'd make it big in Nashville, for whatever he set his mind to, he usually succeeded at. But not this time, and she thought it disappointed her more than him that he didn't. She spoke her thoughts. "Do you have any regrets?"

David studied her intense face for a moment. "I'm not sure what you mean . . . regrets."

"You know, about not being the country singer you've always dreamed of."

"Oh, that. Nope, can't say as I have, Patti. I gave it an honest try and found it wasn't all I'd hoped it would be. Life on the road isn't for me. But teaching and molding young minds is. Not every kid has a father, and they need that role model, if not possible in the home, then at least in a classroom setting. But enough about me. What about you? What are your plans now that you've come back?"

"I'm going to take care of you."

David lifted a skeptical brow. "I intend to make a very fast recovery. And after that?"

Tricia shrugged. "I don't rightly know. Maybe I'll get a job at the cafe. However, if the place is no busier than it was this afternoon, they won't need extra help."

"You must have a greater goal than that." When she made no comment, he changed the subject. "How was New York?"

Again that distant shrug.

"That bad," he mused. "And Mom. How is she doing?" he asked, avoiding his father's eyes.

"You wouldn't recognize her. She's dyed her hair red and lost twenty pounds. I think she's living out her fantasy in the big city." Patti blew out a little sigh and rolled her eyes. "At least that was before I showed up and cramped her style."

Her eyes stopped when they came to rest on the fruit basket on the dresser. David noticed. "Help yourself. I can only eat so much."

She walked over to it and took him up on his offer, choosing a shiny red delicious apple. Tricia read the card—it was from his students. Must be nice, being appreciated, she thought as she noisily bit into the fruit. She chewed a moment, then said, "You'll never guess who else came back to town today."

"Then you'd better tell me."

"Abbie."

His grin faded. "Kenan?"

"Of course. That's the only Abbie I know." Tricia looked at him curiously. "I thought Daddy told you she was coming back."

"No." He looked at his father, a bit disappointed. "He didn't."

Bill smiled languidly. "It's no secret, son. You weren't

Yesterday's Dream 27

in church last week when I announced it, and it just must have slipped my mind.''

Sure, Dad, he thought, then said, ''I assume she's staying at Chestnut Hill.''

''That's right. You sound awfully interested . . . again,'' Tricia teased.

David tried to hide his annoyance behind a tight smile. ''I'm interested, yes, but not for the reason you think. If Abigail's going to be here long enough, perhaps she can sub for me at the school so Lucille can continue with her plans to go on to Florida.''

''I guess she can't say more than no.''

''Which I'm betting she won't. Don't forget, Dad, your congregation was helping to support her during her time in Brazil. I'd say she owes you one.''

''You've got a point there.'' Bill started for the door, then turned. ''I'm going out to the vending machines for a soda. Can I bring you kids anything?''

They answered in the negative and as soon as their father was out of the room, David turned to his sister. ''How did Abbie look to you?''

''I didn't recognize her at first, but then that oversight was mutual; she didn't know it was me either. Abbie doesn't wear her hair long anymore and she no longer has glasses.''

''Little wonder you didn't recognize her. Where did you bump into her?''

''She picked me up along the highway,'' Tricia admitted in a small voice, and David had the response she expected.

''You were hitchhiking?''

''What choice did I have?'' Tricia said defensively, tossing up her hands. ''Someone stole my purse and luggage when I had my back turned and was talking to someone who wanted directions.''

David grunted. ''You were the victim of a scam, little

sister, which put you in a risky situation. At the very least, you could have phoned Dad to pick you up.''

''Yeah, after I talked someone into giving me change to make that call.''

''Well, I'm just thankful it was Abigail who happened by and not some predator.''

The nurse entered at that point, her eyes resting a moment on Patricia. The teen got up from the edge of the bed. ''I'm Tricia Rossi, David's sister.''

David's eyes twinkled in mild amusement. ''Tricia?''

''Patti sounds too much like a little girl,'' Bill offered, catching the conversation as he entered the room with his can of soda. ''Since she's all grown up now, she prefers to be called Tricia.''

''I hate to break this up,'' the nurse continued in a friendly upbeat manner, ''but visiting hours ended ten minutes ago. It's time for David's medication so he can sleep comfortably for the night.''

''We were just ready to leave anyway. Sleep well, David, and we'll see you tomorrow morning,'' Bill said with a fatherly pat on his arm.

And as the nurse was helping her patient into bed, David's thoughts were on Abbie and his ambivalent feelings concerning her. His last thought before falling asleep was that she had hurt him far worse than the surgeon's knife ever could have.

Chapter Three

Abbie awoke to the sound of a light knock on her door. "Come on in," she called out, pushing herself into a sitting position and stretching her arms over her head in a sleepy yawn.

Ruby entered with a large silver tray. "Good mornin'. Your mama thought you'd like breakfast in bed for a change."

"Oh, Ruby!" she beamed. "I don't think anyone's served me breakfast in bed since I came down with the flu, and that had to be a good ten years ago."

"Then it's high time you indulged yourself." She set the tray gently on the bed. Then she lifted the domed lid. "Pancakes smothered in maple syrup. They're just the way you liked 'em when you were a little girl, served with a slice of ham. Then there's toast, coffee, and orange juice too, squeezed fresh, not from a carton."

"It looks delicious. Thank you, but you shouldn't have gone to all this trouble."

"It's no trouble. Besides, I can't do this for you much longer, not with you getting married in a week. My oh my, you'll be a married lady soon, imagine that. A doctor's

wife, just like your mama. Mrs. Abigail Mackel . . .
Mackel . . .''

"MacIlhaney," she offered.

"Why'd you have to go and fall in love with a man
whose name I can hardly pronounce?''

Abbie leaned back against the lacy, propped-up pillows
and laughed. She'd forgotten how much she'd missed this
woman who was never afraid to speak her mind. "Then
call him Doctor Mac. Most folks do."

"Abigail MacIlhaney, that's still a powerful mouthful.
But I suppose I'll get used to it. I know one thing for sure.
I'm lookin' forward to meetin' the man that captured your
heart. He must be very special."

"Oh, he is! Jamie's a profoundly kind and caring man.
Sometimes . . . sometimes I don't feel I'm worthy to be his
wife."

"Not worthy?" Ruby sounded offended, her hands going to her ample hips. "Honey, you'd be worthy of some
real-live prince."

Once again, the woman's statement, said in an air of
seriousness, made Abbie laugh. "Ruby Brown, you are
biased."

"You bet'ya I am." She nodded toward the tray.
"You'd better stop talking and eat before them pancakes
get cold and gummy. Your mama will be ready to leave
for morning services in a half hour and you know she never
was one to be kept waitin'."

Fifteen minutes later, Abigail slipped into a peach-
colored suit which she'd left home in her closet six years
earlier. The skirt hung a tad big around the waist, but the
jacket, which had been snug, now was a perfect fit. As she
combed her hair, her thoughts turned to Jamie. He was
every mother's dream mate for her daughter. Abbie knew
her mother was looking forward to this marriage, even

Yesterday's Dream   31

though she had yet to meet the man. She had sent plenty
of photographs of him home, with letters filled with tidbits
of their work together, educating and healing the Indians
who lived in the Amazon Basin.

Abbie touched the spot on her cheek where Jamie kissed
her every evening. There had never been passionate
kisses—that would wait for their wedding night. It never
ceased to amaze her that in such a day as this, there were
still men, though admittedly few, who respected a woman
so much. Jamie often said he wouldn't initiate anything
which would lead to places they dare not go—yet. That
desired physical bonding would occur, she assured herself,
at the proper time.

During the morning service, Abigail climbed the car-
peted steps to the pulpit to give a brief report on her work
at the missionary school in the jungle. As she looked out
among the two hundred who made up the congregation,
she was encouraged to see them listening in rapt attention.
She spoke of the rewards as well as the dangers of her
assignment and only touched briefly on her ordeal at the
hands of militant rebels. Afterward, as the members filed
through the vestibule, they shook her hand or hugged her
as she took her place beside Reverend Rossi. The only
down side on an otherwise uplifting service was the fact
nothing had been said about the presence of Patricia Rossi
among the congregation. Abbie couldn't help but notice she
sat in the back wooden pew like a little waif—her eyes
seeming large and sad in a too thin face.

She tried to push her dismal thoughts of the wayward
teen from her mind and prepared herself to discuss her marriage ceremony with the minister as soon as the last of the
congregation went through the door. But as soon as the last
one had gone, his thoughts were on something else.

"Abbie, would you do a really big favor for me?" Then

32 *JoAnn Sands*

he proceeded to go on before she had a chance to ask what it was. "Would you take Patti . . . um . . . Tricia to the mall for some new clothes. I have to go to the hospital now, or I'd do it myself. However," he smiled ruefully, "perhaps this is for the best, as you're in a better position to know what's stylish in women's clothes."

"I'm not too sure about that. I've been out of circulation for a while, remember."

"You're still more qualified than I. Besides, Tricia would no doubt pull the obstinate routine and dislike everything I liked. So, will you do it?"

Abbie nodded. "All right. After not being in any malls for a couple of years, I'm kind of interested myself in what's out there."

"You don't know how much I appreciate this." Reaching into his wallet, he pulled out several bills. "I've only got a hundred and seventy, but that should be a start."

Abbie accepted the cash. "I'm sure we can decide on several really neat outfits for that amount. We'll just have to stay clear of the designer labels, so the dollars will stretch further."

Bill grunted, not sure she could pull that one off. "I'm afraid Patricia's mother has impressed upon her she isn't really dressed unless the label says Versace or Karan."

"Sounds like my work's cut out for me. I'll prove to Tricia that notion simply isn't true."

"What notion?" Patricia asked, walking with little enthusiasm into the deserted vestibule.

Turning, Abbie noted she was wearing the same black miniskirt and low boots she had on when she picked her up yesterday. If this was an expensive designer outfit, she'd rather buy something soft and feminine off the rack at a local discount store. Abbie offered an encouraging smile. "Do you have any plans for this afternoon?"

Yesterday's Dream   33

"Nothing more exciting I suppose than practicing my limited cooking skills on a couple of skeptical subjects."

"Put that on the back burner. How would you like to go shopping at the mall?"

"Cool." But the next moment, her grin faded. "I can't. I don't have any money, remember?"

Abbie fanned out the bills. "Oh, yes you do."

Patricia shook her head, unconvinced. "I can't take your money, Abigail. That just wouldn't be right."

"It's not my money, Tricia, it's your father's. So, what do you say, shall we girls go on a shopping spree?" When the teen still looked unsure, Abbie passed the bills over to the Reverend, though her eyes stayed on the girl. "Well, if you'd rather practice your culinary skills, that's okay. But as for me, I'm still going shopping. There's a few things I need to purchase."

Tricia caught the bills just as her father reached to take them back. "Thanks, Daddy. You deserve a really special supper for this one."

It was almost culture shock for Abbie to see the new mall twenty miles away. She had considered herself lucky to get the barest of necessities in the few stores in the driveable distance from the mission. Wait until Jamie saw this!

At first, Patricia gravitated toward anything that resembled punk clothing. It might be a reflection of the times, of young people being on the edge, but Abbie didn't like it. Still, she was careful not to denigrate Tricia's taste, but steered her to the shops which sold more conservative and classically stylish outfits. She did like the jade silk crepe jacket, tee, slacks, and skirt separates.

Abbie pressed her to try on a long button-front black dress adorned with blue flowers. The graceful fit and flared garment certainly expressed Tricia's softer side. And Abbie knew from the way the teen turned this way and that in front of the mirror, she thought so too.

Abigail counted the bills she'd slipped into an empty bank envelope and found only thirty left. They jointly decided that Tricia needed jeans. They went into another shop and found a pair to go with a stylish orange ribbed V-neck top. Abbie like the outfit so much, she tried on an avocado top with matching jeans. Tricia said she looked like a teenager herself and suggested she keep them on. They both did, then completed their shopping spree at a little eatery, sipping Cokes and munching on chili dogs as they congratulated themselves on the great "on sale" items they purchased.

As Abbie sat across from her at the little round table, she was amazed how a new outfit could transform an out-of-control-looking girl into one of innocence. All Tricia really needed was some guidance and concern from an older woman . . . a mentor, she told herself.

"You look real cool, Abbie," she said, wiping the sauce from the corner of her mouth with the paper napkin. "More . . ." she searched for a word, "approachable now."

"You know," she winked, "so do you. After you get a job and have some expendable income, we'll have to do this again."

When Abbie pulled up in front of the Rossis' residence, Tricia turned and invited her inside. "I want Daddy to see all the neat stuff we bought."

Abigail agreed, although she would rather have gone straight home, but couldn't refuse that hopeful look. Tricia had been brushed aside too often this past year. However, when they entered, the home appeared empty. Tricia laid her bags on the sofa, then turned to Abbie again. "I'm not

Yesterday's Dream

hungry, but I'd better be thinking about what to make for supper.''

''What does your father like?''

Tricia thought a moment, then shook her head. She really didn't know him very well. Abbie stared thoughtfully across the room. Years ago when she used to eat at the Rossis' on occasion, she remembered the chicken corn soup with dough dumplings. It was one of the few things Sheila Rossi could make well. Bill and David raved about it. She had asked for the recipe and made it a few times for Jamie.

''Do you have any chicken in the fridge or freezer?''

Tricia shrugged.

''Let's find out.'' Abbie lead the way to the fifties-style kitchen. It was spotless, though the appliances were out-dated and the white painted cabinets offered limited storage space. She foraged around in the refrigerator, then slid out the freezer compartment beneath. There was an unopened pack of chicken breasts with its expiration date still good.

''We're in luck. Now, if we have the other ingredients, we're set.''

''I already found the celery but we need potatoes, creamed corn, onions, and, of course, flour.''

Tricia located everything within a few minutes except the canned corn. The small pantry offered an assortment of everything but.

''We have to have that. While I cook the poultry, will you run down to the store for a couple cans of creamed corn?''

''Yes, I have an old bike in the garage. I'll use that and I'll be back in no time.''

As soon as she was out the door, Abbie began to get things ready. She would cook the chicken just until it was malleable enough to chop it up into bite-size pieces, then continue cooking it the rest of the way with the vegetables.

36   *JoAnn Sands*

She began to sing softly as she cut a rib of celery and the onion.

From his bedroom, David thought he heard voices. He'd been sleeping lightly but decided he'd had enough. Easing himself out of bed, he wrapped his blue corduroy robe around his pj's, pulled the sash tight, and slowly walked out. His bare feet made no sound along the tile floor and throw rugs. He stopped at the threshold, his supporting hand running along the white tile wall as he watched the woman whose back was to him.

Had his sister not told him Abbie was in town, he would never have suspected it was she. The only thing that was recognizable was that lovely shade of auburn hair and the song she was softly singing. It was a song they used to sing as they sat along the bank of her father's small pond, planning their future together. He'd strum his guitar and she'd sing along, looking deeply into his eyes. They were going to be the country western stars of tomorrow. He shook his head and smiled a rather lopsided, melancholy smile. Funny how dreams at sixteen seemed so attainable, while in his mid-twenties he knew, were just the naiveté of a couple of innocent, star-struck kids. A part of him wished it weren't so. "Drawing in a deep breath, he joined her in the chorus of 'Can't Stop Falling In Love With You.''

Gasping in surprise, Abbie whirled around with the paring knife plainly visible in her hand.

David raised his own. "Sorry. Didn't mean to frighten you and . . .'' He added, noting the tears running down her cheeks. "And I certainly didn't intend to make you cry.''

"You didn't,'' she said, struggling to find her voice. "It's the onions. Onions always make me cry.'' She quickly wiped her eyes but knew she was only making them worse by applying more of the juice to the area.

Yesterday's Dream

David slowly walked across the floor, wetted a paper towel and gently wiped them. "There, is that better?"

Speechless, she stared up at him in disbelief.

Grinning, David was quick to take advantage of the situation. "Why Abigail Kenan, I never knew you to be at a loss for words."

"I . . . I didn't realize you were here," she stammered.

"I knew you were—in town I mean. Tricia told me." He smiled again, wagging his head. "It's still hard to remember to call her that. She's always been little Patti to me."

"She's not a little girl anymore." Abbie's racing heartbeat began to decelerate to its normal rhythm. "I'm anxious for you to see her. I took her clothes shopping today."

"Dad told me you were."

"Then you've caught me at a distinct disadvantage. Tricia didn't tell me you were here." She glanced toward the chicken cooking on the range. "She didn't know what to make for supper, so I suggest the chicken corn soup and dumplings your mom used to make."

"Good choice. It's one of my favorites and it's been a while since I've had it."

"There wasn't any corn, so I sent her to get some while I started the meal," Abbie explained, feeling like an awkward schoolgirl herself. She studied his thick dark hair and teasing brown eyes. The last time she'd seen him, his hair was almost shoulder length and his frame a good bit more slender. "You look different," she said after an uncomfortable pause.

"So do you, Abbie, but the change is definitely for the better. You've gotten rid of your glasses."

"Yes, but I still resort to them now and then when my allergies flare and it's uncomfortable wearing the contact lenses." She ran her hand along the back of her hair, conscious of David's eyes on her and knowing he never wanted

JoAnn Sands

her to cut her hair short. "It's easier to manage in the jungle heat this way."

He didn't try to mask his amazement. "Abbie, I remember when the mere sight of spiders and centipedes used to send you screaming in the opposite direction. The Amazon Basin must be loaded with those things."

"It is, and I still do. Some Amazon bugs are truly awesome—spiders with bodies two inches wide and hairy legs seven inches long. There's wasps with five-inch wingspans. And one particularly revolting individual, known as the rhinoceros beetle, has a body the size of a teacup and a long curling horn. This is bad enough, but the darn thing can fly too. When it hits a window screen, it sounds as if someone had pitched a rock."

"Good heavens, Abigail!"

She waved off his concern and said almost flippantly, "You get used to it." Then she changed the subject from her to him as she surveyed his robe. "Isn't it a little late in the day to be in your pj's?" Abbie'd heard he'd lived a bit on the wild side after she'd gone off to college and he began to chase his dream in earnest. He hadn't been in church that morning . . . a hangover perhaps?

"I just got out of the hospital," he said, dispelling her troubled thoughts. "Today, as a matter of fact. Back surgery."

"Oh?" Her concern shifted to another arena. "I'm sorry to hear that. You should be lying down, shouldn't you?"

"I was, until I heard this familiar little nightingale from my past singing our song. I had to investigate."

"I'm sorry I disturbed your rest."

"I'm not," David said with feeling. He had always thought, when he saw her again, their meeting would be confrontational, as he would demand to know why she had broken off a relationship which had meant so much to him. However, the moment he laid eyes on her, that anticipated

Yesterday's Dream

hostility just wasn't there. But all the warm and cozy feelings were.

Abigail stared up at him, not quite knowing what to say. But further conversation was interrupted when Tricia burst through the kitchen door, holding a small plastic bag of canned goods. "Oh good, I see you two are getting reacquainted."

"You didn't tell me David was here." There was a slight tone of accusation in Abbie's statement.

"You didn't ask me." Tricia pulled out the cans and set them on the counter. "Now, show me how to make David's favorite soup."

David grinned once again. "Abbie, you must be a miracle worker getting my sister interested in cooking and . . ." he motioned to their matching outfits in different colors, "a fashion statement that's positive."

The girl looked at Abbie and smiled shyly. "I guess she's the type of person who has that effect on people."

Tricia was quiet and thoughtful through the meal. She'd been doing a lot of thinking since Abbie picked her up and took her to the mall. She had always looked up to Abigail but forgot just how much until that day. If there was one person she could choose for a sister, it would be this girl. She even seemed to project a soothing effect on her father as well. He seemed more relaxed and conversational. And David—there was no doubt she was having an agreeable effect on him. She watched him watch Abbie as she rose from the table to spoon more soup into his bowl from the large pot on the range.

"This is great stuff! I don't know why it should taste better than Mom's since it's made exactly like hers, but it does."

"I know why. Abbie's added a new ingredient. It's called compassion."

40   *JoAnn Sands*

"Patti," her father admonished, but not without a con-
curring smile.

David would have liked to think that was true, but he
cleared his throat and changed the subject. He'd been wanting to say this for the past fifteen minutes. Now seemed to
be the right time, with everyone in an upbeat mood and
their appetites satisfied. "Abigail, I have a very big favor
to ask you."

She looked at him curiously after he seemed to have lost
his nerve and clearly hesitated. He seldom called her by
her given name unless he was very serious or angry—and
she knew it wasn't the latter. "What is it?" she prodded.
Then she guessed, "Become Tricia's cooking teacher for a
few weeks?"

"Not exactly, but you're close. About the teacher part,
I mean. I was wondering if you could take over for me at
the school for the remainder of the year. We would pay
you, of course."

"How many days are we talking about?"

"Two weeks. We have several snow days to make up,
so we're going into the middle of June. We had a hard
winter and too much time off."

Abbie sat her spoon down. "What about Miss Larson."

"It's true she is substituting for me now, but only because there's no one else available. Suddenly it's occurred
to me that someone else is. Abbie, the kids can relate much
better to a younger, more active woman such as yourself.
You'd be perfect because you're used to teaching multi-
age groups. This wouldn't be that much different. Our
school's only a few years old and we have about twenty
students enrolled. Dad's congregation pitched in and
bought the old one-room school at the edge of town. As
more children enroll, we expect to build an addition and
separate the classes from first to third grades and fourth
through sixth. We have excellent textbooks as well as four

Yesterday's Dream 41

computers which have been donated by a computer company. And best of all, there will be no rhino beetles banging against the windows to distract you,'' he said with a teasing grin which she didn't return. His hopeful smile faded and he went on in a more serious vein. ''I realize I'm asking a lot, considering you've come home expecting to relax after completing your own school term, but it would mean so much to me knowing my kids are in your capable hands.''

Abbie stared at her interlaced fingers for a moment. Would Jamie care? After all, the only reason she returned to Laurel Springs without him was to complete her sketchy wedding plans. Perhaps she should discuss it with him first.

''Well?'' David pressed, breaking into her thoughts. ''Will you do this favor for an old friend?''

''All right,'' she agreed, feeling pressured but understanding his position. ''I'll do it for an old friend.''

''Thanks.'' David relaxed back in his chair. ''That's one less thing I have to worry about.''

''Since you'll be teaching David's kids,'' Tricia went on, scheming, ''perhaps you'd better drop by every other day to give him a progress report and me a few pointers on my cooking. Corn flakes and peanut butter sandwiches and now homemade chicken corn is about my meal-making ability. And David doesn't like the former two.''

''Looks like the Rossi family's going to be indebted to you for a while, Abigail.''

Abbie looked at Bill and smiled, surprised that she was actually beginning to look forward to the double challenge.

When Abigail arrived home, she found Lucille Larson and her mother chatting over a mug of coffee and a plate of pecan pie. She was just the woman Abbie wanted to see.

''It's about time you came home,'' Maggie scolded, not entirely joking. ''Your first full day back and I've scarcely seen you.''

42   *JoAnn Sands*

"Sorry, Mom." She kissed her cheek in an effort to pacify before pulling out a chair to join the pair. "Tricia's a disaster in the kitchen, so I offered to come to her rescue."

"Tricia?" Lucy echoed.

"Patti," she explained once again. "She wanted a more grown-up sounding name."

"And with it," Maggie voiced her thoughts, "I hope she gets a more grown-up look. I felt so sorry for the Reverend this morning. The girl looked like a punk rocker, sitting there in the strange hairdo and leather skirt."

"There's been a big improvement since this morning, Mom. Tricia's not a bad girl. She just hasn't had any positive female direction in her life at a time when she needs it most."

"It's been obvious to me that Sheila hasn't affirmed her from day one. It was Bill's idea to adopt her, though she reluctantly agreed. He felt Patrica would have a better chance joining their family than to be shuffled from one foster home to another. As things turned out though, I'm not so sure it was the right decision. I can only hope she's happy now."

"Who, Tricia?" Abbie asked, rising to pour a cup of coffee, then sat back down.

"No, Sheila," she clarified. "Coming to first principles, I can't understand why Bill ever married her."

"I know. They never did seem right for each other, and it obviously was not a match made in heaven, though heaven knows Bill tried his best to make it work."

Abbie took a sip of coffee, enjoying its rich flavor before swallowing it. Then she turned to the slender woman with henna shoulder-length hair and clear blue eyes. "Lucy, how would you like to go back to retirement tomorrow?"

"I'd love it, but David won't be able to teach for the remainder of the school term; you all know that," she said in her pleasant Southern accent.

Yesterday's Dream

"Yes, I know, but he's asked me to take over if you'll agree to it."

Her face broke into a grin which faded almost as quickly and ended with her shaking her head in stubborn refusal. "I can't let you do that, honey. Your mother told me you've come home to get ready for your wedding. And what a surprise that was to hear! I simply cannot impose on those plans."

"It's not going to be a gala affair, Lucy. Jamie Mac-Ilhaney, my fiancé, doesn't have any family except for a maiden aunt in Scotland. She won't be coming. And our family is pretty small. Our guest list will be limited to the elders and their wives. As far as the gown is concerned, I'll be wearing Mom's. And that being the case, I'll be overdressed with about twenty-five guests to witness it."

"My dream for you always has been to have the finest wedding in all of Haywood County."

"You and Daddy already hold that honor, and I wouldn't dream of taking it from you."

Maggie grunted her displeasure. "Sometimes I wonder how Jeremy and I ever produced such a Spartan child."

"I don't know, Ma, but your future son-in-law thanks you, I'm sure." Abbie finished with a grin, lifting her cup in a mock toast and swallowed more of the beverage.

"How about some of my luscious pecan pie to go with that coffee?" Ruby asked, entering the room.

But Abbie was quick to decline. "I can't, Ruby. I had a generous amount of soup over at the Rossis' and before that, Tricia and I had a chili dog and Coke at the mall."

"Humph! That young'un will always be Patti to me." Ruby rolled her large brown eyes. "That high and mighty mama of hers must have put that fancy name in her head."

"I'm sure it was all Patricia's idea to promote self-esteem somehow." Then Abbie changed the subject, turn-

44 *JoAnn Sands*

ing to the older woman in the periwinkle suit. "Well Lucy, how about it. Will you let me be your successor?"

"If you're positively sure it's okay with you and David."

"I'm positively sure. I want to teach, really."

Ruby turned back from the doorway where she was about to exit and walked over to the table once again. "You thinkin' about teachin' at Mr. David's school?"

"For the final two weeks, yes."

She shook her head. "That's not a good idea."

"Oh? Why do you say that?"

"No special reason. I just don't think it's wise, that's all." Then she left without further explanation.

A short while later, Abbie went in search of Ruby and found her in her room—a large, cheerful bedroom in the back of the house. This she shared with her gardener husband, Ulysses. When Abbie entered, she found the woman sitting in front of her portable TV watching *60 Minutes*.

"Ruby," she came right to the point, "are you afraid this will cause trouble between Jamie and me? Is that why you don't want me teaching?"

Ruby looked genuinely surprised. "No, Miss Abbie, though I suppose it could."

"It won't; I know the man. Then what is it? Why don't you want me in the classroom?"

"I can't tell you why."

"Why not?"

She hesitated. "Because you'll think I'm a crazy old fool if I do."

"Never! Now you've really got my interest piqued, so confess."

"The school's haunted," she mumbled.

"What!"

Yesterday's Dream 45

The old wooden rocker creaked as Ruby rose and shut off the TV. "See, I told you you'd think I was crazy."

"I do not think any such thing, though I would like to know what ever gave you such a notion."

Once again there was that thoughtful hesitation as Ruby evaluated the determined girl who stood with her arms folded across her chest and her head cocked to the side . . . waiting. "Oh, all right, you win. My sister, Wilma, says there's been some mighty strange things goin' on out there at night for the past couple of weeks."

"Like what?"

"Like one night when Wilma was coming home from from work, she took a shortcut by the schoolhouse and heard some powerful strange wailing from inside it."

"Is she sure it came from inside? It could have been a owl hooting in the trees."

"It wasn't no owl and I dare say it wasn't nothin' human. She high-tailed out of there as fast as she could! Then another time a week later, she saw an eerie glow in the window."

"Did she tell David about this?"

"No. It was around the time he had his accident that it began, and he was upset enough without putting this on him yet."

"What do you think it all means, Ruby?" Abbie asked seriously as she settled into the rocker, still warm from the woman's broad body.

"You promise you won't laugh?"

"I promise," she said, crossing her heart.

"I think it's the ghost of Eddie Hogan."

"Who's Eddie Hogan?"

"He lived way before your time, honey. Mine too. My mama used to tell Wilma and me a story about the old school right after the Civil War. Eddie was one of the twenty-six boys who were students at the newly opened academy. He was eleven years old, but his small size made him look only about eight. His size and his thick glasses made it hard for little Eddie to make friends. His grandparents raised him after his mama died, but they didn't understand children.

"One day after a heavy snowstorm, the teacher decided to give the boys a treat and take them for a sleigh ride right after lunch. All the students grabbed their lunch pails to eat—all but Eddie.

" 'My Grandma told me to come home to eat, Teacher,' " Ruby said, imitating a child's voice.

Then she mimicked a man. "That's okay, Eddie, but you must hurry right back. The big boys will have the sleigh ready and won't want to be delayed."

"Eddie's pale cheeks must have glowed as he hurried home in the brisk winter air over the snow. For the first time in his life, he was included. Eagerly, Eddie tried to convey his enthusiasm to his grandmother. 'Grandma, our school's going for a sleigh ride. Ain't my lunch ready yet?'

" 'No Eddie, the soup's not quite ready, so you will have to wait.'

"After Eddie gulped his food, he dashed out of the house, but this delay had cost him his sleigh ride. The big boys saw him comin' and with an impulse for meanness, lashed those horses into a gallop. Poor little Eddie called as loudly as he could, 'Here I am; I'm comin'. Wait up for me!' But they wouldn't.

"Only a few days after the sleighing party, Eddie had taken with pneumonia and died. From time to time over the years, folks say they hear the little boy, crying his heart out, or see a small figure racing across the schoolyard. Now, it appears it's startin' again."

"That's a very interesting story, Ruby, but I'd have to see it with my own eyes to believe it."

Yesterday's Dream 47

"Not me, Miss Abbie. I don't need to see no ghost to believe that Eddie still roams the schoolyard, crying to be loved and included."

"Then if I find him, I'll show him somebody cares."

"You pokin' fun at me?"

"No, I'm not poking fun at you." Abbie got up and wrapped her arms around the woman fondly. "If something strange is going on out there, I do think David should be told. Has he ever heard of the legend of Eddie Hogan?"

"I reckon everyone around these parts has heard."

"I haven't," she reminded her.

"You do now, so be forewarned."

Abbie was heading for the door when Ruby spoke again. "How is David?"

When Abbie turned, her face softened and a dreamy look came into her eyes. "He's the same old David that I remembered . . . optimistic, jovial and a tease. I look forward to spending some time with both him and Tricia."

"Did you talk to the Reverend about the ceremony?"

Her smile faded. "Not yet. I didn't want to bring the subject up in front of David and Tricia. I prefer to speak to him in private. He's such a busy man these days. It doesn't matter, we have plenty of time."

But as soon as Abbie left, the congenial smile on Ruby's round face melted away. What if the love those two once shared wasn't dead but simply misplaced. If that were the case, it would hurt this Doctor Mac terribly, or themselves if they ignored the obvious.

The woman shook her head and sank back down on the creaking rocker. "Ruby, you all stop borrowing trouble. Abbie's gonna marry her Scotsman and David's gonna find himself some sweet little thing to settle down with."

Convincing herself of this, Ruby turned the TV back on. Soon Ukee would return from visiting his parents and they would spend the waning hours of the weekend together. She would ask him what he thought of Abbie teaching in a school haunted by Eddie Hogan. He wouldn't like the idea any better than she.

Chapter Four

Abigail acquiesced to Lucille's request that she get a feel for the class by viewing how things were done. Things were done quietly and in order, and Abbie found the retired teacher to be the same disciplinarian she had been when Abbie sat in her sixth-grade class over a decade ago. Lucille was a staunch believer in stressing the merits of good citizenship and a willingness to learn. The woman could be tough, however, and she had the support of Reverend Rossi and the parents to back her up in her authority role. But she possessed a tender side as well. Abbie noticed that she'd put her arm around several of the children to encourage them. She had the approval of the parents on that matter too. How well Abbie had appreciated the hugs of sympathy when her own little brother died. Even now she treasured the woman's empathy when she thought back over it and felt she understood the pain of her loss. Then as now, Lucille taught in an atmosphere that incorporated the morals and ethics of a past generation, but with up-to-the-minute skills in math and the sciences. The children experienced self-esteem because they did well and were proud of their accomplishments. As Abbie viewed the class

50   *JoAnn Sands*

from the back of the room, it was evident to her that they
shared a common love and respect for their teacher.

While the children were out for recess with two of the
sixth-graders in charge of watching over the younger ones,
Lucille and Abbie shared a cup of coffee from the large
Thermos Ruby had sent along.

"I hope," Lucille said, settling back in her straight
wooden chair, "that when the children leave here for their
next level of education, I've instilled enough moral fiber
into their character so that they can refuse the bad choices
they'll be confronted with. But," she shrugged, a bit unsure, "there will always be some who will live on the edge
and experiment with the forbidden. Young people feel
they're invincible, that nothing really bad will touch them.
They think they're immortal."

Abbie leaned her hip against the sturdy old oak desk and
agreed, thinking she'd better grab hold of the subject and
use it to her advantage. "I wonder," she mused, hoping it
sounded like an innocent comment, "if Eddie Hogan felt
that way, running in the snow and catching his death of a
cold."

"Eddie Hogan?" A worry line creased Lucille's brow.
"Whatever made you bring up the name of that poor un-
fortunate child?"

Abigail took a sip from her plastic cup and asked a question of her own. "You've heard of him?"

"Of course I've heard of him. He's the object of Laurel
Springs' folklore. The school closed a couple of decades
after his death and the building stood boarded and idle until
the Reverend bought it for practically nothing. He and David spend last summer doing most of the work to make it
habitable once again."

Knowing she was veering off the subject, Abbie began
to guide her back. "I've heard talk that some people have
seen what they think is the ghost of the Hogan boy roaming

Yesterday's Dream 51

the grounds at night." But the moment those words left her mouth, Abbie realized how off the wall she sounded. She felt her cheeks grow warm and saw Lucille's brows arch.

"Now whoever told you a thing like that?"

"Ruby," she admitted with a hint of reluctance. "Of course we all know Ruby always did possess a lively imagination."

"Abbie, I'm surprised a smart girl like you would take such talk seriously."

"Well, I don't . . . exactly. Where was he buried?"

The chair creaked as Lucille shifted her slight form. "Right here on the property. The headmaster at the time got permission for him to be buried at the school he loved. There's a wrought-iron fence squaring off his grave at the back corner of the schoolyard. Reverend Bill said he wouldn't have him re-interred as the portion of the property wasn't used."

"So you've never seen anything unusual?"

Unexpectedly, Lucille hesitated.

"What?" Abbie pressed.

"A few nights ago when I was working late, I thought I heard a strange sound . . . like a child crying. I looked outside the building and saw nothing. The moon was full, bathing the area in light, so I'm sure I would have seen movement if there were some. When I came back inside, I thought I had brought along a small container of chocolate pudding to eat after I finished my sandwich. But when I reached in my brown bag, it wasn't there. I'm sure there's a logical explanation."

"Like what?" Abbie queried, wanting to get to the bottom of the matter.

"Like perhaps the wind whistling though the cracks for one and the absentmindedness of an old woman for another. I probably never even put the pudding in the bag—I just intended to."

"Maybe . . . maybe . . ." Abbie relented, sipping her coffee, but she knew Lucille was not an absentminded woman, nor did she possess an overactive imagination. If she thought she heard something out of the ordinary, she had— if she thought she brought a container of pudding along, she did. But before Abbie could turn this matter over in her mind any further, Lucille pushed back her armless chair and rose.

"Recess is over," she stated, ringing a buzzer that alerted the students it was time to come back inside for their last segment of studies for the day. This she turned over to Abigail, while she took her place in the back of the room and proudly watched her former student instruct the class. But the pleasant smile on her lips gradually faded as her thoughts drifted off to the little boy who died so long ago.

"My first day went surprisingly well," Abigail told Jamie that evening as she sat curled up in bed and talked to him on the phone.

She enjoyed hearing his easy laugh, and it was a relief to her that he wasn't upset that she'd taken a short-term teaching position. "I guess you have no choice but to work to pay for these phone calls. There's nothing quite like hearing your voice. I miss you, Abigail, so very much. Miss me?"

"Yes." Though in truth, she'd been too busy to dwell on him as she'd expected she would. "How was your day?"

"Hectic, lass, as usual. A woman from the village brought her little girl into the clinic, sure she had appendicitis. She did have painful muscle cramps. Luckily I noticed two puncture wounds on her finger and deduced she was bitten by a black widow. I immediately injected her with an antivenon and am keeping her here overnight for

Yesterday's Dream 53

observation. I expect a full recovery. I'm thankful you had an interest in teaching young mothers good nutrition to their young ones. Already I've seen a reduction in rickets and anemia. You've given them many good pointers on how to eat better when they don't have much money or land on which to grow their crops.''

"I'm glad if I helped. After all, that's why I came down to Brazil.''

His tone became more tender. "I miss our evening walks under the moonlit sky. I miss reading poetry to you and serenading you with my rendition of 'Oh Love That Wilt Not Let Me Go' on my violin. You were a captive audience in which to indulge my passions.''

"Happily captive. I have a thing for musicians, what can I say.''

Jamie laughed once again, then groaned. "Oh dear, there's someone at the door.''

"Then you'd better answer it.'' She smacked her lips together in a semblance of a kiss. "Good night, Jamie, and take care.''

Abbie heaved a heavy sigh as she placed the receiver back on the hook. Why couldn't she become as excited over the thought of Jamie as he obviously was over her. Absence was supposed to make the heart grow fonder, wasn't it?

"It's just the excitement of being home and starting a new though temporary job,'' she assured herself. But when she fell asleep that night, her dreams were of that other musician—David Rossi, not Jamie MacIlhaney.

When Abbie stopped in at the Rossi residence the following day to give a progress report after school, she found David home alone, staring furrow-browed at a blank TV screen.

"I can think of a dozen better things to do with your time than to stare in a frozen gaze at the set.''

His face became suddenly animated at the sight of the woman in the long denim jumper. "I'm so bored I could chew nails, and I don't mean my fingernails."

"That bad, huh? Where's Tricia?"

"Who? . . . Oh, Patti. She's out looking for a job. She should have been back an hour ago. Dad'll soon be returning from visitation and supper's not even started yet. He's got a meeting tonight so he doesn't have time to wait around. It really hasn't hit me until now how on the go he is since Mom left. She was the church secretary, you know, so he's been filling those shoes along with other duties. Thank heaven Patti's home now or Dad would be burdened even more with looking after me."

Abbie placed her shoulder bag on the end table. "Any idea what she was planning on making?"

"I can tell you what she's not making, and that's the soup. We polished that off last night."

"What time do you expect your dad home?"

He glanced at his watch and grimaced. "Fifteen minutes ago."

Abbie whistled. "Then there's no time to waste. Luckily I know of a really quick meal. Hopefully you'll have the ingredients."

Rising cautiously, David followed her into the kitchen. "It's not right for you to do Patti's work. There were certain stipulations Dad laid down when she returned and she agreed to them. One was that she cook the meals on time so he won't be late for his meetings and appointments."

Abbie opened the pantry and accessed its contents, which had grown considerably since she last had a chance to look. She brought out a bag of fettucine, a can of mushroom soup, asparagus spears, Spam, and milk, and sat the items on the counter.

"What can I do to help, Ab?"

Just then, Tricia came breathlessly through the kitchen

Yesterday's Dream

door. She was disheveled and near tears, and seeing her mentor standing with the can of meat in her hand barely brought a smile to her lips. "Hi, Abbie."

Abbie eyed Tricia's new jeans and groaned. They were mud-splashed and torn. A tiny line of mascara ran down her cheek to her jaw line, and her frizzled hair was capped off with a dry leaf. "What on earth happened to you?"

"Oh, some smart-alecky kids forced me off the road with their pickup, and I tumbled off my bike into a field. I was late for my interview, which didn't matter because they took one look at me and made some lame excuse why they didn't need me after all. I'll never get a job and show Daddy I'm a responsible adult!" she finished with a wail.

Abbie heard the unmistakable sound of an engine roar up the lane and stop. Without wasting another moment, she shoved the pan into Tricia's hand. "Fill it with water for the fettucine. We're having an asparagus casserole, if anyone asks."

Abbie was dicing the Spam to fry when Bill entered. His worn face cracked into a smile as he removed his jacket and draped it over the chair back. "Hello, Abigail."

"Reverend," she acknowledged with a slight nod but a broad smile.

He walked over to Tricia, who was trying to looked totally composed but not quite succeeding, as she salted the water. "What's this?"

"Asparagus casserole."

"I'm referring to this," Bill said, plucking the leaf from her hair, then deposited it in the plastic garbage pail in the sink. He pressed his lips together, looking not very pleased with the situation. "I've seen to it that you had the money to buy decent clothes and you've ruined them already. Tomorrow you put on that new jacket and skirt outfit and I'll take you down to the furniture outlet. They have an ad for a salesperson in this morning's paper.'' He loosened his tie. ''Do I have time to shower and shave?''

''Um . . .'' Tricia glanced surreptitiously toward Abbie who gave her the briefest nod as she fried the meat. ''Yes, I reckon you do, Daddy. Run along and I'll have supper ready for you in a jiffy.''

As soon as he left the room, the girl's brave front vanished. ''I saw that ad too. I wanted to surprise Daddy by landing that job as a salesperson. Only it didn't work. I'd be good at dealing with people. I know how to be polite and courteous when I set my mind to it. I see Daddy doing it all the time, and I know sometimes it's not easy.''

''I'm sorry,'' Abbie said, opening the can of mushroom soup. ''But there will be other jobs.''

''Where? In case you haven't noticed, Laurel Springs isn't exactly a boomtown. And to make matters worse, I haven't got any marketable skills.''

''We'll think of something, Tricia.''

''Like what?''

Abbie shrugged a bit helplessly. ''I don't know yet. Your water's boiling. Better dump the pasta in.''

David invited Abbie to stay for supper and she needed little coaxing to accept the invitation. Bill, she noticed, was very pleased with the meal.

''This is delicious, Patti. Where ever did you get the idea?''

''It was in a magazine,'' she said, avoiding Abbie's eyes. Abigail had told her she had clipped the recipe out of a woman's magazine in hope of trying it when she needed a really quick meal. Then she felt compelled to add an afterthought. ''Abbie helped me.''

Bill smiled at the young woman, sensing it was more the other way around. ''I'm glad to see the kitchen's getting so much use of late. I bought a new range, painted the

Yesterday's Dream

cabinets and laid new tile on the floor with the idea it would be just the incentive Sheila needed to use it.'' He shook his head in a woebegone manner. ''I was wrong; it didn't work.''

''I like to cook, Daddy,'' Tricia assured him. ''And I appreciate all Abbie's done to help me,'' she said, turning to Abigail. ''After I practice a bit more, I want to show off my ability by inviting you over for a really nice dinner some weekend.''

''That sounds like an invitation I won't be refusing,'' she said as she took a forkful of pasta, while David grinned, liking the idea—a lot.

After supper, Tricia scooped out some peach ice cream, and as she placed her father's glass dish in front of him, he looked up at her. ''Tomorrow, before we go for that interview, I want you to do something about your hair.''

The interview! How she dreaded telling him she'd already gone and failed. Instead, she pushed back her shoulders and asked indignantly what was wrong with it.

''It looks like a rat's nest, that's what. Didn't Sheila teach you anything while you were with her?''

Only that I wasn't wanted, she thought, and that I learned right away. ''How would it please you to have me wear it?'' she asked in an exasperated tone, at which Bill looked helplessly at Abigail, knowing he'd unintentionally hurt his daughter's tender feelings.

''We'll experiment, Tricia,'' Abbie offered with little thought. ''I'll style yours and,'' she gulped, finding herself cornered, ''you can style mine.''

''You'll be sorry,'' David prophesied with a teasing smile. But as he slowly ate his melting ice cream, he was reminded anew what an exceptional woman Abbie was— always so attuned to the needs of others. And she looked so appealing in her white short-sleeved jersey and turtle motif jumper. The students could identify with her youthful

58 *JoAnn Sands*

freshness, "How's school going? Are the kids behaving themselves?"

"Yes, they are. I like teaching your students; I like it a lot."

"I hope not too much. I do want my students back."

"You shall have them. I do have other plans of my own, you know."

And he was about to ask just what those plans were when she abruptly changed the subject. "Ever hear of a boy named Eddie Hogan?"

"Eddie? Sure, but whatever made you dredge his name up?"

"He was the kid that others always picked on," Tricia spoke up, not wanting to be excluded from this subject. "Some folks say he walks the schoolyard from time to time."

"Patti," her father quietly spoke her name as he tried to get the very last bit of ice cream from the dish. "You should know better than to put any credence in that old folklore."

"I know, Daddy, and yet something must be going on. Ruby told me the legend soon after I came here. I felt so sorry for him. Kids can be so cruel sometimes when all Eddie wanted was to belong."

"Be that as it may, he doesn't walk the schoolyard," Bill insisted. "I'm surprised at you, putting any stock in such tales. That should be reserved for Halloween parties, all in good fun, of course. And as far as Ruby's concerned, she should know better than doing her part in propagating the story. Now, if you young people will excuse me, I must meet with the elders to discuss some budget changes." He rose, patting his still slender waist. "That was a delicious meal, Patti. I can't tell you how pleased I am with your cooperation."

* * *

Yesterday's Dream   59

After they cleared the table, David asked Abigail to take a walk with him. "I need the exercise," he said with a hopeful smile. But before she could answer, Tricia did. "You go ahead. I can do the dishes myself. After all, you came to my rescue as far as supper's concerned—again."

"The doctor said I should exercise daily, but I don't relish the idea of walking alone. I've been sitting too much today and I'm feeling it now," he confessed.

As soon as they stepped outside, David returned to the unfinished conversation they had been having around the kitchen table before. "What made you ask about Eddie Hogan anyway? You never did say."

"Ruby's sister Wilma claims she saw an apparition around the schoolyard a couple weeks ago. Then Lucille said she heard weeping one night when she was working late after classes were over. In spite of the fact she tried to dismiss it lightly as just her imagination, I could sense that it clearly unnerved her."

"It was probably the wind. Although Dad and I did a passable job renovating the place, it's not perfect. The wind can make strange sounds sometimes, especially when one is alone at night. It triggers the imagination."

"You never heard or saw anything?"

"No, I can't say that I have."

His assurance made Abbie feel better. Things had happened in the jungles of Brazil which just couldn't be explained. Villagers said they were the workings of an evil spirit. Maybe they were, maybe they weren't. Abbie simply didn't know, but she didn't want to assume a spirit, evil or otherwise, was roaming her community.

When they paused in the driveway, Abbie glanced up at the moon, in the early evening sky. Jamie . . . his name popped into her mind and she wondered just what he was doing now. Probably finishing up at the clinic or opening a can of fish.

60   *JoAnn Sands*

It took a moment or two for her to realize that David had said something. She smiled apologetically. "I'm sorry."

"I said," he repeated with an indulgent smile of his own, "that we sure had some great times, didn't we, Ab?"

"We sure did. I remember how we used to sit out by my dad's pond on warm summer evenings, watch the sun go down and sing the Top Ten on the charts. We were going to take Nashville by storm." Abbie chuckled at the very notion. "We were so darn naive in those days. Had anyone told me then, I'd wind up in the jungle, teaching at a missionary run school, I would have told them they were out of their cotton-pickin' mind."

"It seems to have agreed with you. You've grown, Abbie. Your character, I mean."

"It's opened my eyes, I'll grant you that. I've come out of my comfort zone and experienced life as it is in much of the world. The more I give of myself, the more I seem to get in return, if you know what I mean."

"I know exactly what you mean."

The young woman went on, sure that he did. "I've found a deep satisfaction in teaching the underprivileged. I've given children the beginning tools they need to make it in this world. Not only the children, but I'm teaching mothers good nutrition and hygiene so they have a better chance of raising their babies through childhood. I can't believe the applause and recognition I once desired so badly could be more satisfying than this is."

"Isn't it ironic? We both wanted to be entertainers, but through circumstances, went our own separate ways to meet up again, fulfilled, but in a different arena."

David paused, and when he spoke again, his tone had an edge to it. And the hurt he'd expected to feel when they met nudged him at that point. "Why didn't you write to me, Ab? When you first went away to school, I mean."

Yesterday's Dream   61

She turned to search his face. "What are you talking about? I did write to you. You never answered any of my half dozen letters and it about broke my heart."

"Half dozen letters?" he repeated incredulously. "I never got any letters." Then it hit him and he groaned. "Mom. Mom must have taken them out of the mailbox and never handed them over to me. It should make me angry as heck but I guess too much time has transpired to do that."

"Why would she do a spiteful thing like that?" Time or no passing of time, it sure made Abigail angry. And it was hard not to transfer her feeling on him for not being outraged by it.

"She felt it would never work. I'm sure that was because of your Mom and my Dad's past."

Abbie found their conversation more and more disturbing. "What do you mean, their past?"

"I mean that Dad was head over heels in love with your mom at one time. Didn't you know that?"

"David Rossi, that's the most outrageous thing you've ever said. Where'd you get such a notion?"

"Mother told me."

"Sheila told you that? And you actually believed her?"

"In this case, yes. It would explain so much."

Abbie turned this over in her mind for a moment. "You're referring to her dislike for me, right?"

"You're aware of that?"

"I'd be pretty dense not to be. I knew both she and my own father weren't thrilled over our friendship. They were afraid of where it might lead. Daddy wanted me to get a good education and marry a physician."

"Well, one out of two isn't bad."

Abbie bit her lip. What was wrong with her anyway? Why couldn't she just come out and say, "I'm engaged to

62   *JoAnn Sands*

one and we're to be wed very soon.'' Her lips parted to finally tell him but his next statement stopped her cold.

''Parents aren't always right, not when it comes to matters of the heart. Dad never let his true feelings be known to your mom, though he's idolized her since grade school. He felt she'd reject him. After all, she came from the most prominent family around, and it was expected she'd marry a man of means, not the son of a grocer. And she did, though it was a man nine years her senior. I'm sure the hardest thing Dad ever did was to officiate at the marriage of Margaret Bailey and Dr. Jeremy Kenan.''

Abbie stood silent, introduced to a history she had never been aware of. David sighed heavily, then went on, conscious of his father's difficult life. ''Dad met Mom a year earlier when she worked at the Mountain View Cafe as a waitress. He dated her off and on but never seriously. I'm sure it surprised her as much as anyone when he proposed to her the very day your parents married. She jumped at the chance and rushed him to the altar in a matter of weeks, fearful, I suppose, he'd recover his senses and change his mind. The situation didn't help Mom's fragile ego any; she always felt second best knowing he'd married her on the rebound. Her joy over finding out she was going to have me solidified their marriage . . . for a little while anyway. Unfortunately she allowed her jealous nature to overrule when she found out Maggie, her great nemesis, also was going to have a baby . . . you.''

Abbie shook her head sadly. ''Suddenly I find myself feeling sorry for your mom.''

''I know. She was not a happy woman and a poor choice for a pastor's wife. After your mom had Jeremy, Jr, my mom tried to have another child but for some reason couldn't. In an act of desperation to fix his marriage, Dad adopted Patti, but Mom never bonded with her and she well knew it. I'm not sure if she could have, even if Patti were

Yesterday's Dream 63

her own biological child. Mom grew more and more bored and impatient with life in Laurel Springs. She always yearned for the bright lights and city life-style. After you left, I felt I had no reason to stick around here feeling sorry for myself, so I struck off to make a name for myself.''

''Had she only not interfered in our lives!''

''Had we both stayed in Laurel Springs, you know very well what would have happened. We wouldn't have continued our education. We would have married instead. I would have struggled to make a living in the furniture factory to support you and maybe a child or two by now.''

It was on the tip of Abbie's tongue to ask if that would have been so bad. After all, she'd already proved that she could live a frugal life and be content in doing it. But David continued on before she could express her thought. ''I saw Mom grow to resent Dad. She was never cut out to be a preacher's wife; she was too narcissistic for that. She had no empathy for the problems of the congregation. And she was jealous of the women he counseled, even though she was always present at his insistence. Poor Dad, he had to brace himself for unjust accusations after every session. Privately, I think he was relieved when she left him to start her life over with her 'dream man' in New York. But professionally, he was embarrassed. How could a man who couldn't hold his own family together be expected to lead his congregation successfully?''

Abbie considered this for a moment. ''None of this was his fault, and I believe his congregation was wise and considerate enough to know it. Bill's been through a lot. Trials and tribulations either make or break you. In your dad's case, it certainly wasn't the latter.''

''Dad's been through the crucible all right.'' But his father had changed over the past few years. He'd suffered the humiliation of not only a one-time prodigal son and daughter, but the desertion of his wife too. He'd been terribly hurt, and he was afraid of ever being vulnerable to that kind of pain again. William Rossi was a shell of his former self. Maybe others didn't sense that, but David did.

David knew too, that people had a tendency of putting ministers on a pedestal and making them something more than human when they were not. What his dad needed now was a close friend whom he could talk to and confide in without fear of receiving that raised brow. Yes, he needed such a friend, but David, sadly, didn't think he could find one in a community that knew so much about them.

Chapter Five

"Abbie, stand still," Maggie mumbled through the pins in her mouth as she tried to raise the hemline on her wedding dress. They were in the high-ceilinged parlor, where Abigail stood impatiently on the hardwood footstool.

"Mom, can't we do this some other time? I really ought to go over to the school and grade those test papers."

"Why didn't you bring them home with you?"

Abbie knew her practical mother would ask that, so why hadn't she prepared an answer? She couldn't just say, "Because I want to be there in person to see what might have rekindled the legend of Eddie Hogan." Her mom, she knew, put no more stock in that than the Reverend. So she settled for a shrug and a lame, "I forgot."

Maggie glanced up, her sandy brow arched, then removed the two remaining pins so she could speak with more clarity. "If I didn't know better, I'd think you were going over to see the Rossis again."

"I do have to keep them informed on how things are going out at the school. Both Bill and David have a vested interest, you know."

"Indeed, and I hope that's where his interest stops."

65

66 *JoAnn Sands*

"Whose?" she asked innocently.

"David. Need you ask? I haven't forgotten the crush you two had on each other, and the passing of time doesn't always erase that."

Abbie paused, her mind awhirl with all the things David told her last night . . . shocking things. Was her mother really as much in the dark as she? "Mom, remember when I first went off to college, I told you I wrote to David several times but he never wrote back?"

"Yes, I remember. Why?"

"Apparently Sheila intercepted those letters. Anyway, he never received them."

"Oh? I'm sorry, Abbie, but hindsight tells us things have worked out for the best. You were able to keep your mind on your studies."

"Was I? I never had closure, Mom. And when you wrote and told me David had left Laurel Springs to pursue his dream, I felt betrayed. That was our dream."

"Oh, honey." Maggie sank back on her knees and looked up at her daughter. The look of hurt was as fresh and raw on her expression as if it had just happened yesterday. "It was a dream that turned into a nightmare. David broke his father's heart, living a life-style that was far from how a minister's son should live." She grunted. "Quite frankly, I don't think it bothered Sheila one iota. She always lived her life vicariously through her son and was more disappointed when he came home, a failure in her eyes. She had told everyone he would be the next Garth Brooks or something like that. But he didn't and that's what embarrassed her."

"Thankfully David didn't sit home licking his wounds but went off to college, and this time he didn't fail."

"That's right, and he graduated with top honors," Maggie said with a note of pride that Sheila should have felt. "Meanwhile, back home, Patti tried so hard to please

Yesterday's Dream   67

Sheila. Sometimes I think that's why she dressed so outrageously. She wanted her adopted mother's attention but never got it. However, she did get Bill's. He was mortified. How could he preach with any credibility how others should live when he had no control over his own family?''

''That was then and this is now. His children have come back, wiser I think.''

''I know David has, but I'm not so sure about Patricia. I think it was a case of having no other place to go.''

''I'm trying to help her, Mom. I can't take the place of Sheila, nor would I want to, but I can be a big sister to Tricia. A mentor, if you please.''

''She's very fortunate to have a friend like you, Abbie. No wonder Jamie loves you! And just wait until he sees you in this form-fitting dress. You are a vision! Kind of makes me wish I were a blushing bride once again.''

''You're still young, Mom. Too young to go through the rest of your life single if you'd rather not be.''

Maggie hummed thoughtfully, then changed the subject as she rose to her feet. ''There, I think I have that pinned evenly. I'll have Ruby stitch it up for you. If you were having a more formal wedding, you could wear the detachable full skirt and train which was made for it. Our guests told me they've never seen such a beautiful gown.''

''Mom?''

''Hum?''

''Is there a man in your life?'' Abbie pressed, not willing to let the subject drop.

''Is there a reason behind this question?''

''Well, I think you have so much to offer the right person. It seems a waste for you to be shut away in this big old house with only Ruby and Ukee for company. This place was meant to be filled with children.''

''To begin with, Abbie, I'm not twenty-four. It is up to you and Jamie to fill the halls with the patter of running

68   *JoAnn Sands*

feet. And I'm scarcely shut away. I do work three days a week and sometimes more if there's an emergency. And lastly, your father and I had a wonderful marriage. I have no interest in sharing my life with another.''

"But Daddy would want you to. If you found a good man to marry, of course,'' she was quick to add when she saw the shock on Maggie's face. "Statistics show that people who have had happy first marriages find their second satisfying as well.''

Margaret arched a suspicious brow. "Abigail, what is all this foolish talk about remarriage anyway?''

Abbie shrugged nonchalantly. "Well, you know how it is, Mom. A woman in love wants those closest to her to be too. Spread the joy, you know.''

Maggie accepted this and questioned her no further. "I felt so special when I married your father,'' she said with a reflective smile. "It was as though I were the only bride on earth. And when I found out I was going to have you and later Jerry, well, I can't describe the feeling. Oh, Abbie, I want so much for you to experience those emotional highs. But more than anything, I want my little girl to be happy. And how can she not be? Marrying a real-life hero who saved her life,'' she finished, running the back of her hand affectionately along Abbie's cheek.

"I love you, Mom,'' she said and a moment later, mother and daughter embraced. But while Maggie was smiling through misty tears, Abbie's expression grew pensive. She was marrying a hero. So why wasn't she weeping with joy like her mother?

Much later than Abbie would have liked, she returned to the rural school and graded her students' spelling papers, giving several of them a colorful sticker for a perfect score. There was no sound . . . no hint of a weeping child, no creaking floor boards or eerie shadows. Still, Abbie had an

Yesterday's Dream 69

uneasy feeling. It was the same sensation she had had in the jungle when unseen eyes were watching her and she and her students were taken captive. She could feel it now as she stared unblinkingly at the sheet of animal stickers. A sixth sense warned her she was being watched. Turning out the lights, she sat in the darkness, her hands folded on the desk before her, and waited for her vision to adjust to the gloom before moving. Moments later, she cautiously made her way to the window and looked out.

Nothing.

What was she expecting to see in that schoolyard anyway? "Abbie, you're letting your imagination get the best of you. Now stop it," she told herself as she closed her attaché case, locked the door, and walked out to her car.

Abbie had herself convinced this Hogan business was nothing but innocuous folklore when she cast a casual glance to her right and froze. There was someone hurrying away from the building to the far end of the property in the little stand of pines. More curious than frightened, she took off too. Abbie ran past the row of orange swings to the fenced off area. The moon cast its shadows, revealing the person—a child, disappearing and reappearing through the pines.

"Wait!" she yelled. "I won't hurt you. I only want to talk!"

Abigail paused a moment, visually canvassing the area, not really expecting a reply and not receiving one either. The moon disappeared behind a cloud. She reached for the iron gate to enter the burial place, but it was padlocked. One lone granite stone dominated the small area. She stood there for several minutes, her hands clasped around the narrow upright bars constituting the fence, watching and waiting, but she saw nothing more. The child seemed to have vanished from the earth . . . or under it.

"You haven't scared me off by a long shot, Eddie,"

70 *JoAnn Sands*

Abigail called out, for want of a better name. "We'll meet again, but on my terms next time," she finished with more confidence than she felt. On an impulse, she took a chocolate bar from her shoulder bag and balanced it on the fence. She never knew a youngster who could resist chocolate. Then she walked back to the car and got in. It wasn't until she turned on the ignition that she realized her hand was shaking.

As David watched his video again, those memories of Abbie returned with even more intense, bittersweet feelings at each successive viewing. Abbie was the first girl he ever kissed, the first one he ever hugged and cuddled and shared his hopes for the future with. It was their future which he expected to be linked both professionally and privately. Her seeming rejection had hurt him so badly that he convinced himself he didn't want her in his life after all. And for six years he'd had himself convinced of that, only to now find out it had been a big misunderstanding—thanks to his meddlesome mother. But in a sense he was as much to blame. Why hadn't he simply swallowed his pride and written to her at college? No one would have intercepted his letters there.

David silently shook his head, telling himself it was counterproductive to dwell on the past. The future was where it was at. Their lives had taken a detour, but perhaps he could get it back on track. He glanced at the phone at his elbow. Perhaps she was free this evening. Perhaps . . .

The telephone suddenly rang, startling him. He reached for it before it could ring twice. "Rossi residence. Good evening."

There was a pause. "Pastor Rossi?"

"Sorry, he's not here right now." He hesitated, unsure. "Abbie?"

"Yes, this is she."

Yesterday's Dream   71

David grinned. This must be meant to be! And that gave him boldness. "What a coincidence. I was just about to call you. I was wondering if you have any plans for this evening. If not, would you like to go up to the Mountain View Cafe for dinner? Becki Bartlett will be singing at eight."

"Becki Bartlett," she repeated. "Oh, yes, I do remember seeing her name on the sandwich board outside the cafe. Have you ever heard her sing? Is she any good?"

"Yes to both questions. Actually, we used to sing together professionally years ago. She's still chasing her dream, and I'd like to give her a little moral support. Will you come along, Abbie? I know you'd really enjoy her singing; she has the gift of connecting with her audience."

Abbie didn't have to think that one over. She'd love to see the woman who teamed up with David after they parted ways. "Yes, I think I would like that."

"Great! But there is one little problem."

"What's that? Oh." It hit her almost right away. "You're not allowed to drive."

"Unfortunately, no. Would it be much of an imposition if you drive? I'll pay for dinner if you supply the transportation to get us there."

"You've got yourself a deal, David."

"What time can I expect you?"

"Give me fifteen minutes to get myself together and I'll see you in twenty."

Abbie hung up to find Ruby standing in the doorway, and she didn't look very happy. "I thought you were going to call the minister about marrying you and Doctor Mac?"

Abbie's smile faded, prompted by a tender conscience. "I did but he wasn't home."

"And David obviously was. Honey girl, do you think it's right to go out on a date when your fiancé will be here in a few days?"

"This isn't a date, Ruby. This is dinner out with an old friend. I think it's going to take more than a few minutes to convince you of that, Ruby, and I really don't have the time." Abbie skirted around her to head for the stairs. "I've got to get ready. When Mom returns, tell her not to expect me till late in the evening."

Ruby shook her head mutely, not liking it a bit, and was sure her mother wouldn't either.

David was waiting on the front porch when Abbie arrived, and a few moments later, they were driving up into the hills in comfortable companionship. Companion . . . good and trusted friend, Abbie told herself, trying to ease her nagging conscience. Jamie would not begrudge her spending an evening with the son of her minister. They had so much to catch up on. She hadn't had a chance yet to tell him of her upcoming marriage, and it bothered her that she hadn't spoken to Bill about officiating at the services. She did try tonight again, but it seemed he was always off somewhere.

At that instant, each spoke the other's name. Then there was the accompanying joined laughter. "You first," he invited with a surrendering wave of his hand.

"It's not urgent," she said, her eyes fixed on the road. "What did you want to say?"

"I was just wondering how school's going?"

She heaved a sigh. "I've been wanting to speak to you about that."

"Problems?"

"Yes . . . maybe . . . but not in the way you would think."

"What is it, Ab?"

"It's not a what, it's a who. Eddie Hogan."

David was silent for so long that Abbie took her eyes off the road to glance at him. He sat with his arms folded,

Yesterday's Dream   73

staring straight ahead. "Well, aren't you going to ask me about him?"

"I was waiting for you to tell me. Just what exactly did you see?"

"I saw a child running from the schoolyard to the stand of pines. He seemed to disappear in the graveyard. I . . . I left a chocolate bar for him on the fence, and when I looked the next day, it was gone," she finished quietly, feeling foolish.

"I don't know who you saw, Abbie, but I can assure you it wasn't who you thought. It was more than likely some kid snooping around where he shouldn't have been and ran when he realized you'd caught him."

"But I didn't 'catch him,' that's the problem."

"If he persists in coming around, you will, or I will. You can count on that. You know me when I put my mind to something."

"Yes, I know you. I remember all too well those foolish dares I'd put you up to when we were children, and you'd always take me up on them to prove a point."

He laughed easily. "I've grown up. I'm not so quick to put myself in an impossible situation."

Abbie put on her blinker and turned into the parking lot. They entered the restaurant, which was considerably more busy now than the day she and Tricia were there. But their table was empty and the hostess led them to it. As David helped her off with her light jacket, his hands froze for a moment.

"What is it?"

David unzipped his own jacket and showed her. He too was wearing the blue country western shirt she had bought them for their last Christmas together, though his was faded several shades lighter from repeated washings. Taking her jacket, he went over to the rack to hang them up, then eased out the chair to seat her. She looked up at him with a twinge of wonder in her eye. "You still have that shirt, after all these years."

"I couldn't part with it. I believe if Mom realized it was you who'd bought it for me, it would have disappeared long ago. I suppose I'm equally surprised to see that you still have yours."

Abbie dismissed his remark with a light shrug. "I was going through my closet for something appropriate to wear for the evening and came across this."

"And you have your locket on again, I see."

Abbie glanced down and fingered it affectionately. "It's my favorite piece."

"It can't be because of its monetary value. I didn't make very much pumping gas in those days."

"The best gifts don't always carry the highest price tag," she said with a shy smile, then picked up the menu to make her selection.

After finishing a satisfying meal of char-broiled steak, baked potatoes, a large salad and coffee, David led the way to the double doors at the back of the building. The words COUNTRY KNIGHTS were in neon overhead.

"That's what the original group was called that started the country western evenings," David explained. "No one ever changed it, though the group has long since broken up. Now they have a different vocal or musical group traveling the circuit. Becki has a gig here for a few weeks, so I'm glad for the chance to hear her."

The room was dimly lit, noisy, and smoky. Abbie would never have come to such a place on her own, but she felt safe with David. There was a heavy oak bar with an ornate mirror behind it. It was from here that people were bringing pitchers of beer to the individual tables. David led her to one close to the stage, then went for two frosty glasses of root beer.

Yesterday's Dream

Abbie looked at it doubtfully as he thumped it down on the red and white checkerboard cloth. "I don't know, David. I'm quite full."

"We'll be here a good hour. I'm sure you can manage to get it down by then. Besides, you'll feel out of place if you're not drinking something when everyone else is."

An hour, she thought, feeling a pluck of guilt. She should be calling Jamie before that.

Perhaps ten minutes passed before a shapely, tousled-haired blonde in a sequin and fringe outfit walked out on-stage. There were whistles and catcalls from the audience, their enthusiasm made even more boisterous by their consumption of adult beverages. Uncomfortable at first, Abbie soon lost herself in the music she and David once privately played and enjoyed. She tapped her toe to the beat of "Singing the Blues," while David mouthed the words to "Half As Much." Becki Bartlett was brimming with talent from the top of her platinum hair to the tips of her leather cowgirl boots. At the last song before intermission, she turned and looked directly at David, who had assumed up until that moment that he had blended in with the crowd.

"I see a dear old friend is in the audience tonight—David Rossi. Davie and I go back a few years when we used to travel the country music circuit together, performing in clubs like this. We were known then as the Bartlett Pair. Honey, could I indulge on your kindness to come up here and sing a little number with me? For old time's sake," she encouraged with a beckoning hand and broad smile.

All eyes turned to the man she was speaking to, and David felt like sliding under the table. Instead, he turned a pair of stunned eyes on Abbie. She smiled weakly. "Go on if you want to," she whispered, not knowing what else to say. He was in a bind.

"Come on, David, don't be bashful. I've got an extra

guitar so you can strum right along with me. We'll sing the song we always used to finish up with.''

David rose with feelings of ambivalence—the old part of him wanting to rush up there on the stage and the new wanting to rush from the room. Becki was obviously as manipulative as when he walked away from their loose partnership. But was he as susceptible to her charm? Becki gave him an uninhibited hug when he joined her. David felt drab in his faded shirt—like a lowly crow beside a colorful peacock. A stagehand handed him a guitar, and he played a few practice chords before their voices lifted in the song ''I Can't Help Falling In Love With You.''

Once David got started, any nervousness vaporized, and it was as though their nearly six-year lapse had never occurred. The pair held the audience in their grip. There was something electric going on between them, and they sang with such feeling that Abbie found it hard to believe was faked, though she wanted to with all her being.

Becki's in love with him, Abbie thought, saddened by such insight. She wondered just what their relationship was during those months her mother had said David broke his father's heart. When the song ended, the audience burst into wild clapping and whistling. They called for an encore. There was little use in taking an intermission until they'd acquiesced to the fans' demands. They sang the chorus once more, each looking into the eyes of the other, then Becki followed him off the stage to join Abbie at the table.

''Abigail, I'd like you to meet Becki Bartlett. Becki, this is Abigail Kenan, an old friend of the family.''

Abbie dutifully extended her hand. ''It's a pleasure to meet you, Ms. Bartlett. You certainly have a way of capturing and holding an audience.'' She surveyed the entertainer and noticed up close there was a hint of hardness about her mouth and a coolness in her heavily made-up eyes, in spite of the fact she was smiling.

Yesterday's Dream   77

"I'm glad to meet you, Ms. Kenan, though I must admit, David has never mentioned you in all the time we've worked together." She sat down on the captain's chair David had pulled out for her, her eyes never leaving Abbie's.

"Actually, David never mentioned your name to me either, until this evening," Abbie couldn't help counter, then felt a bit catty for stooping that low.

If Becki noticed, she didn't let on, and her forced smile remained. "Do you live in the area?"

"For now, yes. I've been teaching at a mission school down in Brazil for the past two years."

Becki raised an eyebrow. "Ooh, I'm impressed. What made you return to civilization?"

"A personal matter," Abbie said evasively, knowing she couldn't say, "I came home to be married," when she hadn't told David yet. But Becki didn't press her further; her interest zeroed in on David, not that it had ever really left. She rubbed his forearm familiarly. "You haven't lost it, Davie. You still wow them with your music, or should I say, we do . . . the Bartlett Pair."

Abbie rolled her eyes and thought, Give me a break. She reached for her soda and began to sip it, if nothing else to stop herself from saying something she'd later regret. He'd told her once never to call him Davie. It made him feel like a two-year-old. She wondered if he ever told Becki that. The woman went on in an annoying, cooing fashion. "What are you doing with yourself these days?"

"Right now, convalescing from back surgery."

"Poor baby. No wonder you're walking stiffly. When you're not convalescing, what are you doing with your time?"

"I'm an elementary school teacher."

"A schoolteacher? Davie, what a waste of your talent!"

Abbie placed her glass down heavily, scarcely able to keep silent. She looked at him, urging him with her eyes to defend himself. He was using his God-given skills to communicate with his students rather than croon about lost love. Only he didn't explain the obvious to her.

"Be honest," she went on. "Didn't it give you a rush up there when you knew you were connecting with the people?"

David hesitated a moment, then nodded with some reluctance. "Yes, Becki, it did. It brought back memories of the old days."

Satisfied, she reached for his root beer and took several long sips, leaving the imprint of her red lipstick over the end of the straw. "You are staying for the rest of the performance, aren't you?"

"I'm afraid not."

Her shoulders slumped in disappointment. "Oh, Davie, I was hoping we could do another song together. Then after the show, I thought we'd go to some quiet little out of the way place and get caught up on what's new. After you take Miss What's-her-name home, of course."

David tried to hide his embarrassment behind a diplomatic smile. "Thanks, Becki, but my drinks are strictly nonalcoholic these days."

"Who said anything about drinking?" She waited for him to reply, and when he didn't, she went on, determined. "If you should change your mind, I'm using the Mountain View Motel as my home base for the next two weeks. We can chat over the beverage of your choice, only don't drop in before ten a.m. I am a late sleeper. Remember?"

The three rose in unison and Becki leaned close to run her artificial nails through his thick dark hair. "I liked it better longer. And I miss your mustache; it used to tickle." Then before Abbie's startled eyes and before David could stop her, she kissed him full on the lips. Without another word, she turned and walked back up on the stage.

David avoided Abbie's eyes as he helped her on with

Yesterday's Dream   79

her jacket and they walked out of the building. He didn't say anything until they were in the car and heading back toward Laurel Springs. "Abbie, I don't know what to say. I'm sorry sounds too simplistic."

"You're right, it does," she agreed, tight-lipped.

He drew in a deep breath and tried again. "Look, I know Becki can be a little forward . . ."

"A little?" she cut in, her eyes beginning to flash. "Try revoltingly. David, half the time she acted as though I weren't even there and the other half she was demeaning and insulting. Why didn't she just wear a big sign saying, 'I'm available.' And to think you actually dated that creature?"

"Yeah, it is kind of funny, a nice boy like me doing a stupid thing like that."

"Don't make jokes about it. I'm serious."

"So am I. You left me, Ab. My world fell apart so I coped as best as I could by going through a period of rebellion. Simple as that."

Abbie accepted his explanation, then asked, "Did you bring her home for your father to meet?"

"Are you kidding? You don't bring home a woman like her, especially when your father's the minister."

A smile cracked Abbie's scowl as she imagined such a meeting with the staid, family-oriented minister. "He'd wonder if you lost your senses."

"No, Ab, he wouldn't wonder, he'd know. David and his Delilah."

Now Abbie laughed, the tension breaking. "That's Samson."

"I know that, but it fits. Samson wasn't too wise. David of old was; he chose Abigail, a woman of wisdom beyond her years. And beautiful too, I bet." He looked over at her and saw the laughter that was on her lips fade. He motioned up ahead. "Pull in that scenic overlook."

Abbie did as told but kept the engine running.

"Aren't you going to turn off the ignition?"

"No."

"If you're afraid of getting chilly, I can take care of that," he said, draping his arm around her shoulder, but she drew back.

"David, please don't."

"Why not? We used to come up here after teen club and kiss under the stars. You never said no then, remember?"

"Of course I remember," she said, removing his arm. "But we're not teenagers anymore."

"You bet we're not. I'm a man and you're a woman, and I find myself more attracted to you than ever. The obstacle before was our education. Well, that's behind us now, so we're free to let our relationship grow and mature into something we could only dream of before. What do you say, kiddo," he finished with a playful wink.

Abbie looked away. "I can't, David. I'm not the same woman I was when I left here six years ago."

"Of course you're not. You've worked in the jungle for a couple of years, survived a kidnapping at the hands of some crazy rebels, and who knows what else. Abbie, I'd like to hear about it. You've been strangely quiet concerning your life down there."

Tell him about Jamie, her conscience urged. He's opened the door to the subject. Tell him if it hadn't been for Jamie, you probably would have suffered horribly at the hands of those two men . . . perhaps even been killed. Be honest and tell him why you can't reciprocate to his longed-for kisses. But when she began to speak, the subject was Becki, not Jamie. "Just what kind of a relationship did you and this Becki have?"

David groaned, passing a wearied hand across his forehead. "So that's it. Becki's the problem. I apologize and

Yesterday's Dream 81

am very sorry for the way she behaved. It was inexcusable. I had wanted this date to . . .''

''This wasn't a date,'' she cut in, once again tight-lipped.

He gave her a sideward glance. ''Maybe it wasn't to you, but it sure was to me. If a guy asks a girl out to dinner, I'd call that a date. What would you call it?''

Abbie ignored his question and asked one of her own. ''Then why did you bring me to a place where you'd meet your old girlfriend . . . so she could outright flirt with you?''

David didn't deny she had been his one-time girlfriend, but he went on trying to convince her of something else. ''I'd have to be out of my bloomin' mind to want to date her. She's got as much substance as cotton candy. Abbie, what must I do to prove to you I don't want Becki. I want you. I think I've always loved you and I believe the feeling's mutual. I am right, aren't I? Well . . . aren't you going to answer me? Or am I to take that as a yes?''

''It's too late, David. Ruby was right, this was a bad idea.''

''Ruby? What's she have to do with this?''

''Counsel of the wise.'' Abbie shook her head and fought back the tears as she put the car in drive. ''I must get home. I'm expecting a phone call tonight, and I have a busy day ahead of me tomorrow.''

David slumped back in his seat. It would do him no good to argue now, but he wasn't about to let this matter drop either. Not by a long shot.

Chapter Six

Bewildered, Jamie MacIlhaney looked out the window at the black-shuttered, rambling white-frame building, then back to the stocky driver. His fair, heavy brows wrinkled with uncertainty. "There must be some mistake here."

The man twisted around and looked at his fare beneath his own gathering frown. "You said you wanted 215 Chestnut Hill Road, and this is it." Still Jamie remained seated, unconsciously tapping the bouquet on his knee. "Look," the cabbie continued, "the meter's running and I haven't got all day. Shall I drop you off, or do you want to go back to town?"

"No. This is where I'm to be . . . I suppose." He dug into the pocket of his outdated tweed jacket and pulled out a scuffed wallet. "What do I owe you?"

The man told him and Jamie settled his account, keeping his opinion of being overcharged to himself. With the large suitcase in one hand and his free arm cradling a couple of bouquets, Jamie started up the brick walkway, his eyes never once losing their awe. Can this be? he kept wondering. Could the woman who lived in the mission complex possibly have come from a house like this?'

82

Yesterday's Dream 83

The door swung open and any lingering doubts melted away. "Abigail!" His thin tanned face broke into a wide grin. Quickening his pace, he took the porch steps two at a time and entered through the door she was holding open for him. His arm ached from the load which threw his lean body off center, and he quickly put the heavy suitcase down.

"Abigail!" he said again, smiled at her beaming face, then bent to kiss her cheek. "For a moment I thought the cabbie had delivered me to the wrong address. Never did I expect to find you in such a place. It's so big! You own the whole house?"

Abbie laughed. There were times Jamie appeared to be a giant taking on the world, and at other times he seemed like a little boy discovering the world for the first time. This was definitely an instance of the latter. "Yes . . . well, Mother does," she clarified at last.

"The entire house?" he repeated incredulously.

"Yes, Jamie, the entire house."

At the sound of another voice, Jamie turned to the woman who was advancing down the hall with her hands outstretched. Catching his free one, she closed hers around it. "Welcome to Chestnut Hill, Jamie. I'm so glad to finally get to meet you."

"Thank you, Mrs. Kenan. But the pleasure's all mine, let me assure you."

"Call me Maggie. After all, we're soon to be family." Her eyes shifted to the showy bouquets he was holding.

Jamie felt uncouth, standing before this pretty woman in a light pink suit, waiting for the obvious. Clearing his throat, he lifted one of the bouquets. "I bought each of you these from a flower shop at the airport. Mrs. Kenan . . . um . . . Maggie, this is yours," he said, placing hers in her hands.

"Botany is Jamie's hobby and a truer connoisseur you

couldn't find. He didn't choose just any old flowers, Mom. They have a meaning. The blue periwinkle signify early friendship, the yellow jasmine stands for elegance and grace, and the sweet basil means good wishes—a very appropriate choice.''

"How sweet! Thank you, dear," she said, rising up on her toes to kiss his cheek.

Blushing, Jamie turned to Abbie. "And these are for you, Abigail. Let me tell your mother what they mean. The dwarf sunflower is for adoration, the oak leaves for bravery, and the white and red roses mingled together are for unity.''

"Thank you, Jamie," she said feeling shy and self-conscious as she kissed him lightly on the lips.

"Such a romantic!" Maggie exclaimed, profoundly happy with her daughter's choice. He lived up to her expectations and more. Though he wasn't exactly handsome—his features were a bit too bony and angular for that—there was something very likeable about his crooked, closed-lip smile and the twinkle in his brown eyes. His hair—of the same color but twinged with shades of red when the sunlight hit it—was somewhat wavy and hung just below his ears.

"Like Abigail said," he continued, breaking into her thoughts, "my hobby is botany. I've found studying the history of the meaning of flowers to be a fascinating diversion from the stress of my daily work. For instance," Jamie said, "in the 1600s, in what is now Istanbul, flowers gained specific meanings that allowed lovers to convey messages to each other without having to write or talk. The language of flowers was introduced to Europe by Lady Mary Montagu, a celebrated letter writer and society poet, who in the 1700s accompanied her husband to the Turkish Court in Istanbul. From there, she sent a letter back to England which interpreted the meaning of some plants, flow-

Yesterday's Dream

ers, and spices. The wonder of flowers, she proposed, was that words and messages of lovers, even altercations, could be passed in a refined and subtle manner without 'inking' the fingers,'' he expressed, rubbing his together. ''Even the positioning of the flowers to the right or to the left had a special . . .'' His voice trailed off and he looked appealingly sheepish. ''Sorry. I'm prone to get carried away in my enthusiasm.''

''If one doesn't have enthusiasm, how can one expect to generate an interest in others? I look forward to learning from you, Jamie.'' Maggie glanced at her daughter with a look that said, I'm deeply impressed.

At that point, Ruby joined the amiable trio, not able to resist the urge to meet Abbie's beau a minute longer. She had watched him unfold himself from the back of the taxi. Now Maggie handed both of the bouquets to her. ''Ruby, please put these in vases and set them on the table for us to enjoy while we eat.''

''Yes, Ms. Kenan.'' She looked at Jamie, who was once again caught up with the house in which he found himself and she couldn't help but grin. ''What's the matter, Doctor Mac? Didn't you ever see a plantation house before?''

''Only in magazines, ma'am.''

''I described it to you,'' Abbie reminded him with a grin.

''Aye, so you did, but words didn't do it justice. It's so big.''

Ruby's grin turned into outright laughter. ''You should have to clean it. Then you get a real appreciation for big. By the way, I'm not ma'am. I'm Ruby Brown. I was Abbie's nanny when she was a baby; now I'm in charge of keeping the place spotless.''

''A formidable task.''

''Yes, but one from which I don't shrink. Ukee, that's my man, he takes care of the grounds, which is no small

86 *JoAnn Sands*

task either. Abbie's told us a lot about you, Doctor Mac. You all don't mind if I call you that, do you?''

"Most folks do. If you don't mind me saying this, I like your accent.''

"Our accent?'' Ruby shook her head hopelessly. "Honey, you're the one who talks strange in this house.''

He grinned disarmingly. "MacIlhaney is Scottish.''

"So is Kenan, but it's a whole lot easier to prounce.''

"If you say it phonetically, it's not so bad. Mac-ill-han-ie.''

The little group laughed again, and when they sobered, Maggie addressed Jamie once more. "You've had a long trip and I know you must be tired and hungry. Abbie'll show you to your room where you can relax awhile before dinner. But don't get too comfortable. We'll be eating at six-thirty sharp.''

Without further conversation, Abbie took his hand and lead him out of the foyer, into the living room and up the grand staircase. She stopped in front of a closed door. "This will be your room during your final days of bachelorhood. Hope you like it.''

Jamie stepped almost timorously over the threshold, his eyes wide as they fell on the curtained mahogany bed. He tried to take it all in at once—the ceiling-to-floor windows, the needlepoint chairs and intricate settee at the foot of the bed. He could only stare.

"Is it suitable?'' Abbie asked when he was silent so long.

Now he found his tongue as he turned and looked at her. "Suitable? Oh lass, it would be suitable for the Prince of Wales. But I feel it's a bit too much for the likes of me.''

"You're wrong, Jamie. It's about time you enjoyed some of the finer things in life.''

"Aye, a part of me would like doin' just that, while the

Yesterday's Dream   87

other part of me is fearful I'd be spoiled. Whose room was this anyway?''

''My parents. Daddy's den, which adjoins this one, is right over there,'' Abbie said, pointing to a door. ''I think it was his favorite room. He'd spent many free hours in there, studying the latest medical journals. And that reminds me,'' she said, taking him by the hand once again. ''There's something I want to give you.'' She took him into the den and nodded to the medical bag on the desk. ''Mom and I talked it over and we think Daddy would have liked you to have it.''

His long tapered fingers caressed it almost tenderly. ''I don't know what to say, Abigail. It's a beaut!''

''Luckily you both have the same first initial but you'll have to change the last one from a K to an M.''

''No, I'll just add the M. Kenneth is my middle name, so it will be J. K. M.'' He looked at her and smiled that boyish, close-lipped smile. ''Thank you, Abigail. I will treasure it always.''

''I can't think of another person I'd rather see using it than you, and look.'' She unzipped it. ''It's well stocked with instruments. Your stethoscope, blood pressure kit, tongue depressors, osocope, and that gizmo. I have no idea what it is.''

Jamie picked it up. ''It's a McSwain Hart. It's used to inflate a collapsed lung.'' He heaved a troubled sigh. ''Had only I had one of these when Delores was hurt, I might have been able to save her.''

Abbie's hand closed over his in an expression of comfort. She never knew Delores, for she had met Jamie after his fiancée was killed in an accident. But through Jamie's colorful descriptions and anecdotes, Abbie felt as though she had known the raven-haired nurse. It was she who introduced Jamie to her love of flowers, and Jamie in turn, had passed that passion onto her.

JoAnn Sands

The quiet couple turned at the sound of advancing footsteps. It was Ruby. "I brought your things up, Doctor Mac. Ms. Kenan said to feel free to take a shower if you like, but be downstairs in twenty minutes. We'll be eating in the dining room."

"The dining room? Isn't that usually reserved for special occasions?"

"I can't think of a more special occasion than welcoming a new member into the family."

As soon as Ruby closed the door, Jamie turned to Abbie, disbelief etched on his face. "I have this feeling I'm dreaming all this and I'll soon wake up in my army surplus cot several thousand miles from here, deep in the jungle."

Abbie playfully pinched his arm. "Hey!" he jumped, startled.

"See, you're not dreaming."

"No, I suppose I couldn't dream anything this spectacular." Jamie encircled his arms around her waist and looked into her eyes. "Have you made the arrangements with your minister yet?"

Abbie's smile froze, then she shook her head. "I tried, but he's at a retreat and won't be back until the beginning of next week."

"What if it doesn't suit him for Tuesday evening?"

"I'm sure he will as Tuesday's usually a free evening. Tomorrow after school we'll see about getting you a new suit or renting a tux."

"I'm a mighty lucky man getting a bonny woman like you as my wife."

An unsettled sigh escaped her lips. Of late she wasn't sure how worthy she was taking him as her husband. She'd made very little progress on their wedding plans other than getting her dress altered. Abbie disengaged his hands from around her waist and gave them an affectionate squeeze.

Yesterday's Dream 89

"I'll give you some time to freshen up now. See you at dinner."

Jamie waited until she latched the door quietly behind her, before sinking down on her father's leather swivel chair. It felt as foreign to him as a throne. His eyes came to rest on the family photo and he picked it up. "You've got a fine daughter there, Jeremy Kenan, and I'll do my utmost to care for her and protect her. And that's a promise."

He sat the picture back down but he couldn't let go of an overwhelming feeling of inadequacy. What would this family man say if he knew his future with his daughter meant spending time, at least another year of it, in a place fraught with danger of every conceivable imagining?

"I don't know if Abbie told you," Maggie said, passing the baked potatoes to Jamie, "that the Kenans came to America from Scotland way back in the late eighteenth century. Malachi Kenan, a physician, settled in the area and founded the town of Laurel Springs. He built this house. My late husband, Jeremy, was the third generation of doctors to live here, and we had hopes that our son would follow in his footsteps but," Maggie shrugged resignedly, "that wasn't to be. The Lord's ways are not always ours."

"Abigail told me her little brother died of leukemia when he was only nine. I'm sorry."

"It's very difficult to lose a child, but I think it's especially difficult for someone in our position. There was this sense of failure. It seemed there must have been something we could have done . . . some treatment we failed to try."

"You know as well as I, we do not have the final say in such matters, Maggie," Jamie said, with a gentleness that brought unexpected tears to her eye.

She mustered up a smile, then nodded. "We nearly lost our Abbie too, but thanks to your negotiations with those

90 *JoAnn Sands*

guerrillas, we didn't. I don't know how we'll ever thank you.''

Jamie blushed, never comfortable with praise. ''The fact that I had taken a bullet out of one of the rebels a few months before gave me the respect and leverage I needed when I tried reasoning with them. Also, it came into play that the two brothers were not well organized, and they understood this was not the way to promote their cause.''

Jamie's long fingers closed over Abbie's and he caressed them. ''You've got a wonderful daughter here, Maggie. She's not only pretty and bright, but she's got a caring heart. Quite a prize for a common man like me.''

He blushed again, this time at his own words, then picked up his fork and dug into the chicken. Throughout the meal, he commented how delicious everything was. It amazed Abbie, after eating the amount that he did, he still had room for peach crumb pie and coffee.

Margaret watched him too, her hands folded and her chin rested on them, her elbows propped on the table. Out of the blue, it seemed, she asked, ''Do you think you would like it here, Jamie?''

''Aye, it's a beautiful house . . . fit for a king.''

Maggie looked at her daughter who sat quietly beside him, her half eaten dessert pushed away. She smiled to her in a conspiratorial manner before shifting her attention back on him. ''Would you like to live here permanently?''

Jamie paused, his coffee cup midway to his lips, then sat it back down again. There was a wrinkle on his brow as he looked into her eyes. ''I don't know what you mean— permanently.''

''I mean just what I said—permanently.'' Maggie lowered her hands to the table and tried to make it plainer. ''I suppose I'm going about this rather clumsily. Abigail told me you're obligated to serve another year in South America.''

Yesterday's Dream   91

"Yes, this is true."

"After that, what?"

"Abbie and I really haven't discussed that."

"It would be nice if you could have a plan for your future before you fly back. Laurel Springs needs a doctor. An urban physician might find this community dull and boring. But not you, Jamie. I think for a man such as yourself, it would be the chance of a lifetime. My husband's office was in this house. I haven't sold much of his equipment so you'll have pretty much what you need to begin your practice. The house is large, as you've seen. You and Abbie would have plenty of privacy to live your lives as you see fit. It's truly a lovely area to raise your future children."

Jamie's lips parted. He could scarcely believe what she was saying. "You want me to take up your late husband's practice."

"Yes. I want you to pick up the baton and carry on in place of his son. I know Jeremy would heartily approve of such a move. And a Scotsman at that; my husband was always very proud of his heritage. And for you it would be a wonderful opportunity."

"Golden." He smiled. Was there no end of the surprises he would find here in this quiet North Carolina Valley?

Maggie rose. "I'll leave you two alone for now as I'm sure you have much to discuss and digest." As she walked by, she affectionately patted her future son-in-law on the shoulder. "Good night, dear."

"Good night, ma'am," he mumbled, then turned in his chair to face Abbie. "Did you know about this, lass?"

She shook her head. "No. Frankly, I'm as surprised as you are, but you know, I kind of like the idea. Mother's right. Laurel Springs is a nice place to settle down and raise a family. And I know you want a family, Jamie. That is one thing we have discussed."

92 *JoAnn Sands*

Jamie grunted in agreement. "And it's certainly safer raising them here than in the jungle where one has to concern themselves with scorpions and snakes."

"You did say after your term was up, you did want to begin a practice in a rural area that doesn't have a physician."

"Aye, that I did," he admitted in his heavy accent.

Abbie grinned, liking the idea the more she thought about it. She'd forgotten how soft and comfortable life had been here at Chestnut Hill. "It's as Mom said. This is a chance of a lifetime."

Jamie nodded, patting her hand absently as he stared off into space. "I suppose a man would have to be daft not to take her up on such bonny offer. But would you mind, lass, if I give it a wee bit more thought before committing myself?"

"I know you're a man who's not prone to making spur-of-the-moment decisions, so you give it all the time you need. I want this to be a decision you can be comfortable living with."

"It's just that this is so unexpected—the house . . . your father's medical bag . . . and now the biggest surprise of them all, to actually set up my future practice here in the valley." Jamie was thoughtfully silent for a long moment, then he addressed her with excitement flashing in his eyes. "Could I see the office now?"

"Follow me," Abbie said as she rose, sensing his decision was all but made.

Chapter Seven

The day had gone well for Abbie. The children accepted her authority and quickly bonded with their perky teacher. Bringing in her father's old microscope, she invited them to look through it at a strand of their own hair, a drop of well water, and a butterfly wing.

In the afternoon, she worked on sharpening their reading and spelling skills, and at the end of the day, when their attention span was waning, they made creative get-well cards for David out of construction paper and bits of material from Ruby's colorful scraps.

After classes had concluded for the day, Abbie phoned home and asked Jamie to bring her a bowl of leftover soup. She wanted to stay over to grade the papers instead of bringing them home. He brought it without question.

Abigail took the lid off the Thermos so the delicious chicken aroma could filter out through the open window, then motioned for Jamie to follow her out. Again without question, he trailed her to the car. She had told him about the supposed ''ghost'' last night and how she wished she could trick him out into the open.

''So, the soup is a lure,'' he guessed.

94 *JoAnn Sands*

Abbie nodded as they stooped beside her auto and out of view from the little fenced off graveyard. "I can't prove it, but I think he comes into the building at night to sleep. There's no lock on one of the windows, and he could put something under to ease it up enough to lift it. I had a geranium sitting on the sill; it's been moved. I think he's been moving around at night to scare any superstitious folk who might see him. The classroom has a trap door which leads to the root cellar. There's no other way in or out. If I were a betting woman, I'd bet you dinner at the Mountain View that that's where he's sleeping or even spends a part of his day."

A look of pity and concern reflected in his soft brown eyes. "Abigail, if this be so, it is no life for a child!"

"If he's willing to exist like that, it must be better than the life he's run away from."

"Then we've got to do what we can to help him."

"Knowing you as I do, I just knew you'd say that." Abbie peeked around the side of the car to the stand of pines. There was no movement. They waited an endless fifteen minutes more, while Jamie chewed his stick of gum and Abbie chewed her nails.

"My curiosity's getting the best of me," she said, slowly rising, but Jamie caught her arm. "We'd better give the lad a wee bit more time."

"I think he's had enough. The aroma of the soup is bound to be too big a temptation." Abbie walked cautiously back to the building with Jamie at her heels. When she looked in the window, her eyes widened. "It's gone!" she whispered needlessly, for he had noticed it as well.

"Aye, and we had a view of the window the whole time. The lad didn't enter, which means he must have been in the building with you all day."

"There's only one sure way of finding out."

Jamie nodded gravely as he took the lead to the door

Yesterday's Dream

and opened it. Together, they made their way over to the trap door, but it was he who grabbed the metal ring and pulled the lid back. Abbie cried out in surprise and jumped aside, while Jamie reacted quickly and wrapped his arms around the child and held him.

"Let me go!" he yelled, kicking and screaming. "Let me go!"

Abbie's hand slipped from her gaping mouth to her pounding chest, her eyes still wide. He couldn't have been more than eight, and a dirtier child she'd never seen. From the top of his hair, which she thought to be red, to the tennis shoes which were caked with mud, he was filthy. His jacket was torn, and the knees of his denim coveralls were wet with earth.

"What's your name?" Jamie asked, totally composed and scarcely batting an eye. It was as though they were meeting under perfectly normal circumstances.

"I ain't saying and you can't make me."

"Feisty lad, aren't you."

"I ain't afraid of you," he said, twisting around to look up at Jamie. Then he glared defiantly at Abbie. "And I'm not afraid of you either, Miss Kenan."

"So, you know my name, do you." Quickly composing herself, she leaned forward, her hands on her knees and looked him in the eye. He glared back without flinching. "You have me at a disadvantage," she said with forced sweetness. "I can't very well call you little boy every time I want to address you, can I?"

"Nope." Then a devilish gleam came into his eye. "But you can call me Eddie."

"Eddie Hogan?" she queried and he nodded. "Yep, that's me. Aren't you scared?"

"No."

Her unexpected reply turned his mischievousness to disappointment. "Why not? Everyone else is."

Abbie folded her arms across her chest and studied him with a disapproving brow. "Actually, you're the one who should be scared. You stole my soup."

He stared back, looking less sure of himself by the moment. "Well, what'ja expect me to do. I was hungry."

"I just bet you were. Haven't had anything to eat since that chocolate bar, have you?"

"You tricked me," he accused with a scolding finger.

Abbie gently pushed it aside. "You gave me no choice. I don't know who you are, but this I do know. You're not Eddie Hogan."

The young woman paused, giving him time to clarify the matter and when he didn't, she went on. "I think the next step is for us to notify the police and turn you over to them. I'm sure they have a list of missing little boys, and ten to one, you're on it."

For the first time she noted a flicker of fear in those bold eyes. "Please don't do that."

"Sorry, but I'll have to if you don't start cooperating and tell us who you are."

"Kevin Martin," he mumbled, his eyes downcast.

"Kevin Martin," she repeated. Good, now they were getting somewhere. "Your parents must be worried sick about you, Kevin. How can we get in touch with them?"

"You can't. They're dead."

"Oh? Then who is your guardian?" she asked in a more empathizing tone.

He shook his head, visibly near tears. "I was staying at a foster home, but please, don't make me go back there. If you do, I'll only run away again."

Her eyes met Jamie's for a moment, then she dropped to her knees to get eye level with the child. "How long have you been living in the root cellar?"

"About a month, I reckon."

A month? she thought. How on earth did he pull it off

Yesterday's Dream 97

so long? Abbie forced herself to smile. "Then I'd say it's high time you've had a cooked meal and a nice soft bed to sleep in, don't you think?"

"Yes, ma'am," he said, the first sign of civility on his otherwise belligerent face. "It has."

"Did you like the soup?"

He nodded. She knew he devoured it quickly, poor kid. "I know where there's plenty more where that came from. Come with me?" she encouraged, extending her hand.

But he held back and looked with an uncertain eye up at Jamie, who was still holding him by the shoulder, however, with a grip he could not wiggle out of if he wanted to. "It's your choice, Kevin. Either Miss Kenan's house or the police. If I were you, I'd choose Miss Kenan's. They took me in too, and I can tell you, a finer house you'll never find."

"Well, okay." He drew up his shoulders proudly. "But that don't mean I'll be staying more than one night."

"I understand," Abbie agreed, letting her breath out slowly. She'd confront tomorrow when it arrived. For now she was content to take one day at a time. The couple left the room in silence, with the reticent child between them.

Ruby stood her ground, her hands on her hips as she shook her head. "Oh no, young man. You aren't comin' to my table until you all take a bath."

"I don't need one."

"Humph! You sure do! And you're gettin' one if I have to scrub you myself."

Kevin whipped around Jamie's legs and tried to get from her reach. "I don't want no bath, and if you don't want me at your table, then I won't come. I'll sit on the back porch and eat."

Jamie gently eased him around so he could place a sheltering arm over the boy's shoulder. "You know, Ruby's right. You do need to be cleaned up before you eat."

Kevin folded his arms stubbornly and stared at Ruby under a pouting lip.

The housekeeper shook her head. "You ain't eatin' in my kitchen lookin' like that. You'd better be cleaned up before Miss Margaret comes home or she'll shoo you right out of here. There's never been a dirty little boy in this house, and we sure as shootin' aren't gonna start now. Enough said. Now quit your stalling and take off those clothes and giv'em to ole Ruby."

"No!" Kevin pressed against Jamie even harder. The man patted his shoulder. "Tell you what, lad. I'm going to give you choice. Either Ruby gives you a bath, or I do. What will it be?"

"That's a choice?" he asked indignantly.

"Sure it is. Her or me."

His eyes fell suspiciously on Ruby, who still stood there with her hands on her wide hips, her head inclined, watching him with a determined gleam in her eye. "Well, make up your mind, boy."

"Ah, there's no real choice here. I'll go with . . ." He looked up at the man quizzically. "What did you say your name was, mister?"

"I didn't. It's James, but everyone calls me Jamie," he said, thrusting out his well-manicured hand.

Kevin hesitated a moment before putting his grubby little one in it. Then, cocking his head, another thought struck him. "You talk kind of funny."

"Aye. I grew up in Scotland when I was a wee lad such as yourself, but now I live along the banks of the Amazon River."

"Wow!" His interest piqued, and his eyes grew enormous. "Do you ever see crocs or fat snakes?"

Jamie nodded, sealing the boy's confidence and admi-

Yesterday's Dream   99

ration. "Only in Brazil, the crocs are called caymans. You must be real mindful where you swim or take a bath. I'll tell you about some of my adventures while we're cleaning up. Okay, Kevin?"

The boy bobbed his head enthusiastically, while Jamie slid his arm around the child's shoulders and winked to Abbie. She smiled back. Jamie had a way with kids in any culture. The sight warmed her heart.

"You and Jamie did what?" Maggie asked, not sure she really understood her daughter's hurried explanation.

Abbie repeated herself, tossing her arms out helplessly. "I didn't know what to do, Mom. We couldn't just let Kevin sleep in that root cellar another night now that we knew he was there. I contacted the child protective agency a few minutes ago and they said they'll be sending someone out tomorrow. In the meantime, I thought he could stay in Jerry's room."

From the frozen look which came over her mother's face, Abbie was sure she was going to refuse outright. Then after an obvious mental struggle, she nodded reluctantly. "I suppose one night won't hurt."

"That's what I thought." Then Abbie pressed further. "Do you suppose he could borrow one of Jerry's tee shirts and a pair of jeans?"

When Maggie showed further signs of inner turmoil, she gently continued. "I know you were unable to part with his things after he died, Mom. You said someday you'd give them to a needy little boy. Well, I think that day has come, for there's no needier child that I personally know of than Kevin Martin. Trust me on that score and I think . . . no, I know when you see him you'll agree. Ruby says she doubts if she can get his clothing clean, although she's in the laundry room as we speak, trying hard. Meanwhile,

100 *JoAnn Sands*

Jamie's up in the bathroom scrubbing his body with hopefully, more success.''

''All right, Abbie, you win. He can't very well come to
the table wrapped in a bath towel. I'll use your good judg-
ment to give him whatever he needs.''

Abbie chose a bright red tee shirt and a pair of blue
jeans, both with their price tags still attached, thinking it
might be less painful for her mother than to see Kevin in
something Jerry actually wore. She also picked out a
change of underwear and white sneakers, hoping they'd fit.
She waited anxiously outside the bathroom while he tried
on the full set of clothing.

Kevin emerged smelling of soap. His red hair was a
shade lighter and he possessed freckles across his nose and
cheeks that she hadn't been aware of beneath all that grime.
He was grinning, his pudgy hands jammed into the deep
pants pockets, which seemed to have been bought expressly
with him in mind. His ordeal behind him, he appeared a
happier, neater child. Jamie, however, had splashes of
soapy water on his khaki short-sleeved shirt. His hair had
edged down his forehead in his physical effort to restrain
and clean, but from the easy, lopsided smile on his face,
he too looked pleased with the end result.

''Well, I declare, Kevin, if you don't look like one cool
dude. Now that leaves the matter of supper. You hungry?''

''Yeah!'' He grinned. ''What are we havin'?''

''A casserole,'' Abbie said evasively, knowing few children favored broccoli. But then, no one made it quite like
Ruby. ''And chicken,'' she added.

That grin grew wider. ''Can I have a drumstick?''

Kevin sat upright, with elbows off the table, as Ruby
spooned the broccoli casserole, potatoes and chicken onto

Yesterday's Dream 101

his plate, never questioning the main ingredient of the casserole, only stating it tasted really good.

"I made plenty," Ruby assured him, pouring iced tea into his glass. "And since you've made such a metamorphosis in your appearance, you can eat all you want."

He grinned proudly across the table to Abbie. "I know what that word means, Miss Kenan. It's when a caterpillar turns into a butterfly. I listened to you teach the other kids while I was hiding below. I learned a lot that way from you and Miss Larson. You all had a captive audience and didn't even know it."

Tears glimmered in Abbie's eyes. "You're right, I didn't know. But I can promise you this, you'll never have to learn that way again. From here on in, you sit in the room at your very own desk with all the other boys and girls."

Abbie stole a glance toward her mother and was touched to see tears glistening in her eyes.

After topping off supper with a dish of chocolate ice cream, they all escorted Kevin upstairs, where Abbie opened the door to a child's room.

The little boy hurried in but stopped abruptly, his eyes growing wide at the sight of the assortment of toys on the bookshelf. Walking over to it, he reached for a shiny red fire truck.

"Kevin . . ." Maggie began. She'd followed him, experiencing that inner struggle once again. He turned, his hand frozen in midair. "Yes ma'am. What is it?"

That was the last gift we'd bought for our Jerry, she wanted to say. Instead, her lips turned back in a stiff smile. "Nothing, dear. If you want to play with it, you may. Just be careful you don't break it."

Abbie watched as he sat it on the floor and moved it back and forth, making a siren-type noise with his mouth.

He looked up at Abigail and stated proudly, "My Daddy was a fireman."

"Really? What happened to him?"

"He died fighting a house fire when I was just a little kid."

"I'm sorry to hear that," Maggie said. "What about your mother?"

"She got sick last year and died too. That's why they stuck me in a foster home. I hated it!" he spit out in sudden emotion. "So I ran away and I'm never going back."

After stating that, he turned his attention back to the fire truck between his legs. "*Vroom . . .*" Kevin said, slipping into his safe, imaginary world once again, while Abbie and Jamie exchanged glances of concern. "*Vroom . . . eeer! . . .*"

Then it hit him. He looked at Maggie, who was watching him with a strange expression on her face. "Mrs. Kenan, who does this room belong to?"

"No one now." She took a few steps across the room and knelt on the oval braided rug beside him. "It used to be my little boy's."

"And the clothes I'm wearing. Were they his too?"

Maggie nodded mutely.

Kevin was thoughtful as he pulled the fire truck up on his lap and fingered one of the metal ladders. "Where is he now?"

"He died of a terrible disease."

He viewed her somberly. "So did my mama. What kind of disease?"

"Something you probably never heard of. Leukemia."

"Yes I did! That's what Mama had."

"Oh." It came out in a broken sob, which she was quick to cover over with a smile. "You must miss her very much."

Yesterday's Dream 103

He nodded. "And you must miss your boy. What was his name?"

"Jeremy, named after his daddy. But we called him Jerry for short."

Abbie watched him watch her mother and she could see he was thinking about their situations. It seemed a plan was hatching in his mind, and Abbie knew she was reading him correctly when he began to speak slowly. "I don't have a mama now and you don't have a little boy anymore. Do you suppose maybe . . ." But his voice died in mid-sentence. He couldn't bring himself to verbalize his desire.

But Margaret knew what he was thinking, and she could feel her shoulders grow rigid with tension. She had to get out of the room. She couldn't bear to consider what he wanted to ask of her. Rising slowly to her feet, she said, "I must get ready for bed now, Kevin, and I suggest you do too. I am a working woman, you know," she added in afterthought as reason for excusing herself so abruptly.

"What do you do?"

"I'm a visiting nurse for the county," she said as she walked stiffly toward the door. She had to get away from this child who was chipping away at her protective wall and getting to her. She couldn't allow that to happen; she could not let herself bond with another child only to have him snatched away. She paused at the threshold but couldn't quite meet his longing eyes. "Good night, Kevin," she mumbled, leaving the room.

Abigail and Jamie stayed with the boy for another twenty minutes, then gave him a pair of Jerry's pj's. Giving him some privacy, they returned a few minutes later to tuck him in. The couple was surprised when he first wanted to kneel at the bed to say his prayers.

"And God bless," he finished, "Miss Kenan and Jamie. And let Mrs. Kenan like me and see that I'd be the perfect little boy to take her Jerry's place, and she my mama's. Amen.''

Abbie glanced over at Jamie and smiled thinly. It would take a near miracle to make the latter part of that prayer happen.

Kevin was upstairs playing with his new treasure trove of toys when Marcella Wells came to see Abbie the following afternoon. She'd led the fiftyish, athletically built woman into the parlor, where Ruby offered her a glass of tea. She declined. So the two women sat across from each other on the matching floral love seats, with Jamie nestled beside Abigail.

Marcella did not attempt to put the couple at ease. She was all business and brusquely told them the home which the ''Martin boy'' had run away from would not be taking him back. The husband had been jailed for drug possession several days ago. ''Would it be an imposition for you to keep him another day or two?'' She went on. ''I believe we can locate a more suitable family by then.''

''It's no imposition. Kevin's a fine little boy.''

Marcella smiled thinly, not convinced of that. ''May I see him for a few minutes?''

''Certainly. I'll get him.''

But when Abbie brought the happy youngster down a few minutes later, his demeanor immediately changed when he saw the social worker. Catching his breath, he pressed his lips together and narrowed his eyes. ''What are you doin' here?''

Marcella cocked her head of dark curly hair. ''I stopped in to see how you're doing, Kevin, and sorry to say, I see you still have that chip on your shoulder.''

''Ms. Wells,'' Jamie spoke to her as he gestured to the child to come to him. The little boy complied. ''Last night,'' he continued with scarcely a pause, ''when Kevin

Yesterday's Dream 105

was taking his bath, I saw some fading bruises on his body as well as some healing cuts. The lad should have been taken from the family who last had him. Better yet, he should never have been put there in the first place. Life had become so intolerable that he found it preferable to live in a root cellar than in a house with a roof over his head. You should be more thorough when checking into placements for these youngsters.''

The woman visibly blistered at his gentle chiding. ''Are you telling me how to do my job, Mr. . . . ?''

''MacIlhaney,'' he offered. ''I'm saying that when you, in a very real sense, are holding a child's life and future in your hands, you've got to be more careful where you assign them.''

''We are understaffed and overworked,'' she said in a controlled tone. ''What do you know about pressure and critical decision-making anyway?''

''Plenty. It's not just Mister MacIlhaney, but Doctor MacIlhaney, and trust me, lass, I do make life-and-death decisions almost daily.''

Marcella's gaping mouth snapped shut. Kevin was quick to pick up on her embarrassment. The impulse to add a few choice comments was just too much to resist. ''Doctor Mac lives along the waters of the Amazon. He visited school today and told us all about it. The upper part of the river is Indian country, and even today, some of the tribes have had no contact with the outside world. There's a tribe that lives there—the Jivaros—who are noted for shrinking the heads of their enemies,'' he said, proud of his knowledge.

Jamie lightly nudged the boy to be quiet, but he was too caught up in the mental pictures of the faraway land to notice. ''I won't go with you, and if you try and make me go, I'll run off to South America with Doctor Mac and Miss Kenan.''

Her eyes shifted to the uncomfortable physician and she

smiled dolefully. "Legally you couldn't do that, but if you could, I can't imagine a more dangerous atmosphere in which to raise an eight-year-old."

"Well, they can't shrink heads anymore," he mumbled. "That's also illegal."

"You got one. You showed it to me this morning."

"It's artificial, Kevin. I thought I explained that to you."

"It looks real enough to me, and I bet Miss Wells would think so too. I'll get it and see if she yells."

"No you're not," Jamie said, catching his wrist with a firm hand when he jumped up from the sofa.

Marcella rose too and gave the child a wicked sort of smile. "Perhaps in Kevin's case, some time spent in the Amazon Basin might be just what he needs to curb his propensity toward the incorrigible."

Kevin didn't know what incorrigible meant, but he liked the idea. "You serious? I can go?"

"Certainly not. You're to remain right where you are, with the Kenans." Her cold dark eyes shifted to Abbie now. "But I'll be staying in touch, and when we find a suitable couple, be it a day or a week, I'll be back to take him off your hands."

"I'm not going! I'm not!" he yelled, jerking himself free from Jamie's now light grasp. The child ran from the room, bumping into Maggie, who was quick to break his fall. She'd been standing in the shadows, listening unobserved for the past few moments.

"Kevin, it'll be okay," Maggie assured him, giving his arm a light, encouraging squeeze. "Things will work out somehow, you'll see."

"How?" he demanded, not accepting words; he wanted action. And when she only shrugged her shoulders helplessly, his face crumbled. "Will . . . will you take me?"

Maggie's heart pained at his pitiful plea. He was reminiscent of Jerry when he cried to her, "Make me better,

Yesterday's Dream   107

Mommie." Now she said the same words to him as she spoke to her son then. "I can't do that sweetheart. I'm so sorry, but I just can't."

"Why not?"

She pointed out the obvious. "For one thing, I don't have a husband."

"You could marry Dr. Mac," he suggested, naming the only man he knew in her life.

"Kevin," she said patiently, trying to reason with a child whose heart couldn't listen. "He's going to be Abbie's husband, you know that."

"But . . . but they can't take me along to the Amazon!" he reminded her, bursting into tears."

"Kevin, please. Calm down now," Maggie commanded as her hands slipped up to his quaking shoulders. "Things will work out for you. I admit, I don't know how, but I feel certain they will."

However, her words of good intention could do little to allay the boy's fears. "You don't want me! Nobody wants me!" he yelled, bursting free, and he darted from the room and up the stairs. The stunned, silent adults heard him bang the bedroom door behind him.

Kevin took the fire truck he'd been playing with roughly and tossed it against the bedpost in a fit of anger and frustration. His rage, which had been building for an hour, had finally come to a head and erupted in this destructive act. Maggie didn't want him; nobody wanted him. He'd now convinced himself of this. Upon impact, the wheel flew off and the little red fire truck fell on the wooden floor with a clatter.

The child cringed and bit his lip, expecting someone to rush in and investigate what the commotion was all about. He began to count slowly to ten. On number nine, the door flew open and he turned to face the consequences, fully expecting to see Maggie, who would scold him for breaking the toy she'd warned him to be careful with. He didn't care. At that point he felt like breaking all of Jerry's toys. He was gone and would never come back. So why wouldn't she let him take his place?

But when the person entered, he found it wasn't Maggie. It wasn't Abbie either, or Jamie, or even Ruby. He gasped, stepping backward and tripped over the throw rug. The next instant he went down hard on his backside, but his surprised eyes never left the frowning face of the black man who towered so tall. "Who are you?" His question scarcely came out more than a frightened whisper.

"Ukee. And I know who you are, Kevin Martin. My wife told me."

Kevin watched suspiciously as he walked into the room, leaving the door wide open while he bent his muscular, overall-clad body to pick up the truck. He hadn't decided yet if this man with a funny name was friend or foe. Kevin's eyes never strayed from his as he slowly rose to his shoeless feet. "I didn't mean to do that."

Ukee inclined his white-haired head and arched a knowing brow. "Oh, yes you did."

The little boy didn't contradict him but asked a question pressing heavily on his mind. "Are you gonna tell Maggie what I done?"

"That all depends."

"On what?"

He smiled but said nothing as his eyes shifted to the floor in search of the wheel. "Oh, there it is," he said, bending his six-foot frame once again to retrieve it.

"Can you fix it?" Kevin asked, suddenly very anxious to have it done.

"Maybe." His attention turned to the bed now as he ran his callused fingers over the fresh nick on the post.

"I'm sorry," he murmured contritely.

Yesterday's Dream   109

"For what? Breaking the toy and nicking a costly piece of furniture, or getting caught red-handed in your fit of anger?"

"Both, I guess. I suppose you're gonna tell on me, aren't you?" Kevin pressed, but to no avail.

Ukee sank down on the edge of the bed. "My mama used to say, 'When you spill anger, you can't always mop it up.' "

Kevin wrinkled his freckled nose. "What's that supposed to mean?"

"Think about it." The man patted the spot next to him. "Come here, son, and sit a spell with ole Ukee."

He waited for Kevin to comply before continuing. "You must have been hurtin' mighty bad to toss that truck the way you did."

"I guess." He sat on his hands and swayed his legs as far as the bedframe allowed. "I don't want to go to a foster home," he admitted at last. "I wanna stay here."

"Well now, I can certainly understand that," he agreed with an easy chuckle. "Chestnut Hill's a mighty pretty house to live in."

"Have you lived here long?"

"Yep," he said with a deep nod. "Ever since I married Ruby, but she wouldn't want me to tell you exactly how long ago that was. That would be sort of givin' her age away, and womenfolk are kind of funny about things like that, you know."

Kevin didn't know, but he liked being included as though he did. The boy grinned, warming to the man. "Ruby's all right, I guess."

"She sure is!" he agreed with an expression that could only be termed, adoration. "And can that woman cook. Says you've been cleaning your plate, and that pleases her. But if you're like I was when I was a boy, you always have room for some candy.'' Reaching into his pocket, he withdrew a root beer barrel.

"Thanks!" Taking the candy, Kevin quickly unwrapped it and plopped it into his mouth. They fell into a comfortable silence for a few moments, then, when Ukee thought the time was right, he went on.

"I know something else too, Kevin. I know how it hurts when you lose your mama and daddy, 'cause I lost mine when I was ten.''

"You did?" Kevin's interest piqued even more. "How?"

"Car accident. I was angry for a long time, wondering why me? Why did I have to be the one to lose my folks ... good, God-fearin' folks ... to be raised by an aunt whose only interest in me was having a farmhand. I worked my fingers to the bone for that woman and her husband and never once got so much as a thank you. As time passed, I grew angry with everyone but Ruby, the pretty young thing that lived on the next farm. She understood me and literally loved the bitterness out of me, but it took a long time.''

"My foster parents were mean to me too. They made me work hard with no time to play, and when I didn't do things to suit them, they'd hit me.'' Kevin was silent for a few seconds. When he spoke again it was with a terrible longing in his voice. "I wish Abbie and Jamie would adopt me.''

"If they did, you'd have to leave the comfort of this big house and go with them, wherever.''

"I don't care. I could be happy anywhere if I were living with nice people. Even Brazil.''

"I believe you mean that, but I really don't think you could do it according to the law.''

"I know, that's what Ms. Wells said.'' His shoulders

Yesterday's Dream   111

slumped as he sighed wistfully. "I don't suppose there's any chance of Maggie adopting me, is there?"

"No, I don't think so. She's not married, and I don't imagine she'd want to tackle such a venture alone."

Ukee could almost see the wheels of thought going inside the boy's head. "But you and Ruby are. Do you think maybe . . ."

Ukee pushed those thoughts from his head as he ran a playful hand through the boy's hair, messing it up . . . then he gathered the truck he'd laid on the striped bedspread.

Kevin dropped the matter and asked for a more attainable favor. "Do you think you can fix it for me?"

He contemplated the matter for a moment. "Yes, son, I think I can. Let me go downstairs for a moment to get my tools."

Ukee walked to the door, then turned and looked back at the boy, sitting twisted on the bed watching him with longing eyes. He wasn't such a bad kid . . . likeable, actually. "You asked me a question a little while ago," Ukee prompted.

"I asked you several questions you didn't answer. Which one do you mean?"

"I mean the one about me telling Miss Maggie you spilled your anger out on her son's toy."

"Are you gonna tell her?"

He grinned quickly, his teeth flashing white. "It'll be our little secret. I'll even touch up that nick so she'll never know of your tantrum, but you must promise to never do it again."

"I promise."

Winking, Ukee left the boy a lot calmer than when he found him an hour before.

Chapter Eight

When Patricia entered the living room, she found her brother watching the home video on TV. Mildly embarrassed at her untimely intrusion, David reached for the remote to turn it off.

"You don't have to stop viewing that just because I came in. That was Abbie on the screen, wasn't it?"

He nodded, then thought, what did it really matter if she witnessed their private moments together? It was history. Obviously it didn't matter as much to Abbie as it did to him. He pushed the PLAY button and Abbie's laughing face came on the screen again. She was sitting by the Kenan pond in shorts and a tank top, her long hair blowing in the light breeze. Picking up a guitar, she began to sing, "Can't Help Falling In Love With You."

"Bet she still does, too."

"What?" he asked, knowing he was letting himself in for it, yet knowing Tricia wouldn't allow him to ignore her teasing.

"Love you."

"Oh, Tricia," He emitted an exaggerated groan. "Grow up."

Yesterday's Dream   113

"I have, in case you haven't noticed," she said, striking a provocative pose.

David waved his hand in dismissal, but couldn't help grinning in the end. "I know . . . I know, you left here a girl, to return a woman, far wiser than her years."

"So, my wisdom makes me wonder why you're not mature enough to admit you still have feelings for the girl."

"You're having a romantic fantasy, Tricia, but don't worry, you'll outgrow it."

"You're the one living in the fantasy world if you remain in this state of denial." She gathered a throw pillow in her arms and hugged it. "I hardly think you would be here, sitting all by your lonesome, watching old home videos of your one-time love if there wasn't more than a smidgen of interest there. I think there's a flame just waiting to be fanned into a fire. Don't you think?"

"I think you've been reading too many of those sizzling paperbacks."

Tricia shook her head stubbornly. "The only thing I read is your body language, and that longing in your eyes. I'd like to have Abbie for a sister-in-law, but I just bet not as badly as you'd like to have her as a wife."

If you only knew, he thought, but he couldn't admit that to her. Impulsively, he pulled the pillow from her grasp and playfully bopped her over the head with it. "I know why you say that. So you can skin out of your cooking responsibilities and have her do it."

"Not true. I have no secret motives. I just like her, that's all," Tricia insisted, grabbing the pillow back and wrapping her arms around it. "King David recognized his Abigail was a special lady and he married her. Somehow, David, you and Ab just seemed meant to be. You were the darlings of Laurel Springs High, remember?"

"Yes, I remember. But that was then and this is now. We've parted ways."

114   *JoAnn Sands*

"True, but your paths have crossed once more. You're enjoying the same careers. That's fate. What must happen, David, for you to make the first move? Have the walls fall down on you? Hey . . ." Tricia interrupted herself, pointing to the screen. "Who's that?"

David didn't have to look to know. "Becki Bartlett."

"Her name sounds familiar. Oh yeah, she's the singer Abbie and I saw advertised at the cafe. You know her?"

"Yep. Not only did I know her, but we sang together for several months during my quote, 'rebellious year.' She's staying at the motel behind the cafe."

"How do you know that?"

"She told me and invited me for a drink—in front of Abbie, no less," he added sheepishly. "We had sort of a date the other night, and I took her out to eat and then to hear Becki sing." He shook his head, still cringing at the thought. "That wasn't one of my better ideas. It turned into a disaster. Becki kept putting her down. She even kissed me as though Abbie wasn't even there."

"David!" Tricia squealed, mortified. "Where in the name of common sense was your brain, taking one girl-friend to meet another. The tension must have been terrible."

"You could have sliced it with a knife."

"So, this Becki person is still carrying a torch for you?"

"It appears so. Had I only known she was going to react like that, I would never have taken Abbie to hear her. She even had me come up on the stage and sing a song—for old time's sake."

"Not a smart move."

"Downright dumb!" he grunted.

"Did you like her at one time?"

"I thought I did, but it was infatuation. Seeing those two women together was like comparing diamonds to rhine-stones. Abbie's quality. Becki can't hold a candle to her,

Yesterday's Dream 115

and if I didn't realize that before, I know it now. Abigail's the only woman I ever truly loved.''

''You're making progress. At least you're finally admitting it.''

''All right, I admit it. But what good does it do me? She's angry.''

''Of course she's angry. No, she's jealous,'' Tricia corrected. ''You took her to see an old girlfriend who had the audacity to kiss you and ask you to her motel for a drink and who knows what else.''

''I don't drink anymore, and there wouldn't have been anything else.'' He looked at Tricia with new hope fluttering within. ''You really think she's angry because she likes me?''

''Oh, David, sometimes you can be such a dunderhead. Of course that's why she gave you the cold shoulder. She's probably as miserable as you are. Call her up and ask her out.''

''You really think I should?''

''Of course!''

But David remembered the way Abbie reacted when he tried to kiss her. She insisted it wasn't because of Becki coming onto him like that. Then what?

It hit him at that point. There was the matter of her capture by the rebels. She obviously didn't want to discuss it with him. Maybe something unreported and awful happened and she was just plain turned off by men. If that were the case, he'd have to patiently remind her that not all men were brutes, if it took him her remaining time at Laurel Springs to do it.

''All right,'' he said at last. ''Tomorrow I'll stop by right after school's dismissed and tell Abbie how I feel. I do love her, Tricia. I suppose that's why I haven't been able to get her out of my mind ever since I found her singing in the kitchen. Thanks for making me face it.''

116   *JoAnn Sands*

Patricia smiled, pleased with herself. "Ah, that's okay, David. What are sisters for?"

"I'll wait for you," Patricia said as she pulled her paperback from her purse and opened it to where she'd stopped reading last night.

David dipped his head next to the open window. "You don't have to."

"Yes I do. Abbie might have something else planned and she won't be free to give you a lift back to the house," she pointed out. "Hopefully though, that won't be the case. And when I know it for sure, I'll gladly leave you two alone to let whatever is to happen, happen." She lifted her thumb up and grinned. "So go for it."

"Thanks. I owe you one, sis." He returned her grin before slowly making his way over to the brick building. As he rehearsed what he wanted to say in his mind, he noticed a little red-headed boy. He'd been entertaining himself on the swing but when their eyes met, he hopped off and came over to him. David lifted a curious brow. He'd never seen this youngster before.

"Hi. You new around here?" he asked, feeling the need to start the conversation.

"Yeah, kind of I guess. I go to school here. Miss Kenan's my teacher."

"Oh? You like her?" he asked, but thought it was strange she hadn't mentioned anything about a new student—especially strange since it was the tail end of the school year.

"Yeah," he said again, looking bashful as he lowered his head and kicked a loose stone with the toe of his sneaker. He looked up again and decided he wanted to talk to this stranger. "I'm waiting to go home. I hope they're ready soon cause I wanna go out and play. But first I want to have a big wedge of Ruby's peach pie with Ukee."

Yesterday's Dream   117

By now David's smile had faded completely. "You know Ruby and Ukee Brown?"

"Sure. I'm stayin' at Miss Kenan's forever, unless"— he wrinkled his freckle-splattered nose—"Ms. Wells find me another foster home to go to like she threatened to."

"You're staying with Abigail?" he said, trying to make sense of it all.

"Yeah, I told you that. I'm staying with Abigail and Doctor Mac."

"Doctor Mac?" he echoed, passing his hand across his forehead in a confusion he didn't try to mask. "Wait a minute here. Abigail Kenan I know, but who is this Doctor Mac?"

"Abbie's fiancé."

His hand slid down over his neck and hung there like a hook. "Her what?"

"Fiancé," he repeated, parroting the word Maggie had used when she explained why she couldn't marry Jamie. After Ukee had fixed his spill, she had come into his room and spoke gently to him, telling him Abigail and Jamie would soon marry and they would like him to be their ring bearer.

"Abbie doesn't have a fiancé," he said in a sharper tone than intended.

The confident smile on the little boy's face faded. "Does too. He's in the schoolhouse with her now. I came outside so they could hug and kiss if they had a mind too. Grown-ups like to do mushy things like that. Yuk!" He finished by wiping his mouth with the back of his hand.

Normally a statement like that would have made David laugh, but not now. He snapped his gaping mouth shut and started for the door, forgetting about his sore back. His only concern was to dispel this terrible rumor. He heard the child yell that he couldn't go barging in on them, but he ignored him and threw the door open.

118   *JoAnn Sands*

Abbie was sitting at the desk while a tall slender fellow whom David had never laid eyes on before, was massaging her neck. And worst of all, they were both laughing, obviously enjoying the act. David could see nothing humorous.

"Just what the heck do you think you're doing, mister?"

Jamie's long, immaculate fingers froze on Abbie's shoulders. She gasped. "David! What are you doing here?" she countered back, no less surprised than he.

David closed the door on the prying eyes of the child and took a few steps closer. "This is my school; I have a right to be here. So what's his excuse?" he asked, gesturing to the man who appeared to be measuring him as much as he was the man. He looked a bit older than David, with a slight graying at the temples of his wavy, light brown hair. He could use a haircut, David judged, as strands of hair brushed his turtleneck. That black sweater and the tweed trousers he was wearing seemed vaguely familiar, David thought as he took a second look. Then it hit him. "Hey, those are Doc Kenan's clothes you have on!"

Abbie rose, dreading this meeting she knew would eventually come, though she'd hoped it would be under circumstances she could control. Not like this. "David, this is Doctor Jamie MacIlhaney, and yes, he is wearing Daddy's clothing. I gave them to him as he had so few warm clothes with him since he lives in Brazil. Today's unusually chilly for this time of year. And Jamie," she said, looking up at the man whose stare was still locked with David's, "this is David Rossi. As he said, he runs this school."

Jamie was the first to gather his composure. He offered his hand along with his close-mouthed smile. "Nice to meet you, David."

The man can remain civil while stretching the truth, I'll give him credit for that, he thought as he stared at Jamie's outstretched hand for a long moment. Then to Abbie's re-

Yesterday's Dream 119

lief, he grasped it, albeit reluctantly. "Doctor Mac-Ilhaney," he acknowledged with thinning patience. "What's going on here, anyway?"

At that point, Kevin, whose curiosity had gotten the best of him, opened the door and entered. He'd heard David's question. "Doctor Mac lives in the jungle," he said proudly as he joined the tense trio and draped his arm around Jamie's waist. "He knows headhunters and natives that shoot poisonous darts at people," he exaggerated, becoming carried away with his own mental visions. "And he can wrestle an alligator and he even saved Miss Kenan and her class from some nasty old gorillas," he went on excitedly, visualizing the animal variety.

David stared, unblinking. He didn't know whether to catch his breath in shock or laugh at the absurdity of it all. But then he did remember that Abbie had been taken hostage by guerrillas. "Is that a fact?" he said, more impressed than he was willing to let on. "You must be a real-life Crocodile Dundee."

"Hardly. The wee lad's got quite an imagination, although the part about me negotiating with those guerrillas is true."

"Just what is your relationship with Miss Kenan?" David asked, but he knew. Kevin had told him the unthinkable, which now didn't quite seem so.

"We're informally engaged, but she has agreed to become my wife very soon."

"And I'm gonna be the ring burier," Kevin said exultantly, mispronouncing the honor. But the group was too preoccupied to care.

"Your wife," David echoed, and all the fight seemed to go out of him. "Well, I suppose I can't blame her for falling for such a brave man. The scariest thing I ever faced was back surgery."

"David . . ." she began, but he turned to her and cut her

off. "What I can blame you for is the fact you never told me about MacIlhaney. Abbie, I always thought you were the most honest and caring woman on earth. Guess I was wrong about that. Turns out I never really knew you."

Abbie flinched visibly, but she willed herself not to cry, though her eyes burned with the threat of tears "I'm so sorry, David. I wanted to tell you everything, but the time never seemed quite right. I never, never wanted to hurt you."

"Well you have." David started for the door, then turned to give her a final look. "You know, right now Becki looks pretty good. At least with her I know exactly where I stand." And with that, he left the room, banging the door behind him.

Abbie watched, feeling torn. She wanted to run after him and beg him not to go to Becki on the rebound, that in the end she would only bring him even more heartache. But her duty to Jamie was stronger. She had fences to mend with him. But how? She'd unintentionally wounded two good men.

When she turned to Jamie, he was bending over Kevin, speaking in a calm though authoritative tone. "You'd better go out and amuse yourself on the swings for a while."

"But I'm tired of swinging."

"Then take a few runs down the sliding board. Please, lad," he went on when Kevin just stood there, looking up at him with a worried brow. "Do as I say now. Miss Kenan and I must talk in private."

"You're not gonna fight, are you?" he asked suspiciously.

"No lad, we'll not fight."

Satisfied, the boy left them alone. Abbie took a deep breath, steeling herself for whatever was to come.

"This Mr. Rossi," he began the second they were alone.

Yesterday's Dream

"You obviously mean a great deal to him. Just how good a friend are you?"

"We were high school sweethearts. Were, Jamie, *were*," she emphasized.

"Maybe from your standpoint, but not from his. I'd say he fancies you still are."

"I don't know why he should," she said, not quite able to look him in the eye.

"I don't know why he shouldn't, when you didn't consider me important enough to tell him about us."

Abbie looked up, her vision blurred with hot, unshed tears. "Oh, Jamie, that's not fair. You are important to me. You're going to be my husband."

"Precisely." His hands settled on her shoulders, and though his touch was light, it felt like a terrible burden to her. "Then why didn't you ever tell me about him."

"Because David was my past," she explained lamely. "You're my future."

"But we're both in your present, Abigail, whether you like it or not." His eyes dropped to the oval locket which hung at her breast. "You always wear that; you have ever since I've known you. Once you commented that a special friend had given it to you for your birthday. It was David, wasn't it?"

"Yes."

"Open it."

"What?"

"Open the locket, Abigail. I must see whose picture you carry close to your heart."

"Oh, Jamie, has it come to this? Don't you trust me?"

"Open it, or I will."

Reaching up with shaky hands, she unclasped it. Her father's smiling face was on one side and Jamie's was on the other.

His shoulders slumped as he expressed a sigh of relief. "I'm sorry, Abigail, but I had to know."

"Now you do."

Jamie's arms slid around her back and he drew her against him in a fierce hug, quite unlike his manner. Still, he was hurt by Abbie's incomplete honesty. He'd been totally up-front with her concerning the Brazilian nurse who'd died only weeks before they were to marry. Yet this woman who'd now grown so dear to him had said nothing about the teacher who had once been such an important part of her own life. And judging by his reaction, she was still a part of his, if even in his own deluded mind.

The hands of the kitchen clock were positioned at a minute after midnight when Abbie entered the room. Though her body was bone-weary, her mind was racing over the troubling events of the day. Hoping it would help her sleep, she made herself a glass of warm milk and nibbled on a graham cracker. Laying it aside, she delved into the pocket of her robe for her oval locket and opened it up. She stared at Jamie's picture for a moment before carefully removing it. Behind was a picture of a fifteen-year-old David, his hair slightly long, his grin youthfully optimistic.

Suddenly Abbie looked up, startled by the footstep. It was Ruby, following Shadow. She opened the back door to let her out, then turned to Abigail. "You can't sleep," she guessed.

"No."

She grunted. "I was sleepin' just fine till Shadow woke me up wanting to do her business."

Abbie smiled, knowing the dog preferred sleeping in her room. She'd always been the closest to the housekeeper, and the woman reciprocated by taking charge of her daily needs. Abbie placed Jamie's picture on top of David's, hoping the older woman wouldn't notice. But Ruby seemed

Yesterday's Dream

very attuned to affairs of the heart, a fact Abbie found both comforting and disconcerting. At this instance, she found it more the latter.

Dragging out a chair, Ruby plunked her ample form into it. "You've got yourself a problem, don't you, honey?"

Abbie shrugged noncommittedly. "I'm in love, Rube, if you consider that a problem."

"I sure do, when you're in love with two different men at the same time. I'd say that's a very big problem."

Abbie drew back, annoyed. "That's the most ridiculous thing you've ever said."

"No it isn't. Thinkin' Kevin Martin was really Eddie Hogan was." She said this with a smile which teased one from Abbie's lips. Then she sobered and continued. "You're engaged to marry one man yet find yourself still in love with the other. Now be honest enough to admit it, Abbie."

"Okay, okay, I admit it." Why pretend with this woman who'd literally known her since the day she drew her first breath. "I've hurt them both and I'm miserable for it. That's why I can't sleep. And I wonder if I ever will be able to again."

"Now who's making ridiculous statements?"

Abbie leaned forward, her elbows on the table as she tried to make her understand. "David's had so much disappointment in life. First he loses his dream of becoming a country singer, then I left him, and finally, his mother deserts him. Had I only known she'd kept my letters from him, I would never have severed all ties. Now, years later I discover his interest in me has been rekindled. I didn't know how much until this afternoon when he found Jamie and me together at the school. The look of shock and betrayal tore into me like a knife. I hurt him and . . . and I hurt Jamie." She smiled languidly. 'Whoever wrote the lyrics to the song about hurting the ones we love must have written them from personal experience. Jamie is such a good man, one in a million.''

''I know he is, but you haven't married him yet.''

Abbie pulled back, stiffening. ''I don't know what you're implying.''

''Oh, yes you do,'' she challenged, understanding Abbie's heart like no other. ''You can't fool old Ruby.''

''The wedding will go on. Jamie too has suffered loss, don't forget.'' She paused to take a sip of her cooling milk. ''And he saved my life. I don't think I'm being too melodramatic when I say those children and I probably wouldn't be here today if it weren't for his savvy. Now, after years of thankless work in the jungle, he's offered an opportunity to get out and inherit Daddy's practice. The folks in this area will take to him; I just know they will. He has the type of personality that draws people to him. He'll be a huge success. He deserves the chance, Ruby. He deserves the chance at the prestige and bank account that comes with being a successful doctor. Don't you agree?''

But before she could answer, Shadow scratched on the door to be let back inside.

Jamie twisted and turned, entangling his legs in the sheets, unable to sleep. He couldn't get Abbie from his mind, hurt that she'd never spoken of David. Tossing back the covers, he got out of bed and turned on the light. He'd caught his reflection in the antique mirror and took a few steps closer to it. He was clothed in Jeremy's silk pajamas instead of his own underwear, sleeping in Jeremy's comfortable massive bed in place of his own iron cot. And now he had a chance to step into Jeremy's once lucrative practice. Mr. Cinderella, that's me, he thought with a touch of wonder and amazement. Then why am I not jumping with joy?

Descending the stairs, Jamie went down to Jeremy Kenan's office and entered through the ''secret'' hall door.

Yesterday's Dream

He flipped on the lights and wandered about in his bare feet, touching the furnishings and admiring the latest in equipment. It was so much better than the antiquated stock he worked with now—infinitely so! What an opportunity! A person would have to be a fool to pass it up. But he had to be sure of Abbie's commitment to him. Pressing his hands together, he brought them against his chin in a stance of meditation and thought and thought. Some time passed before he turned off the lights and left.

Jamie was about to return to his room when he became aware of voices and saw the light lit in the kitchen. He slowly walked down the hall. Though staying well in the shadows, he listened curiously when he heard his name and noted the passion in Abbie's voice when she spoke.

When he was settled beneath the covers a short time later, he could still hear her voice replaying in his mind and he thought, Yes! I do deserve it. After ten years in the jungle, I deserve to get paid for my efforts. I saved Abbie's life and now she is giving back to me. A man would have to be a fool to let this pass, he assured himself. The matter finally settled, he rolled over and went to sleep.

''But Abbie, you have to come, you just have to.'' Patricia argued her point as she stood in the foyer of the Kenan home.

And once again, Abigail shook her head. ''I don't think it's a very good idea, Tricia. You have to know what happened at the school the other night.''

''Of course I know. I was waiting in the car for David and he told me all about it—though not until later that night. He had to sulk in silence for a while first.''

''If you know what happened, then you surely can understand that I can't go to your place for dinner on Saturday.''

''Yes you can,'' she insisted. ''David won't be there if

he knows you're coming. Besides, I owe you a meal.''
Tricia's gaze shifted to Jamie, who'd joined them. He'd
placed his hand companionably on Abbie's shoulder, and
Tricia had to force herself to ingratiate herself to them,
though now she spoke to the man.

''Abbie was caring enough to teach me to cook. I'd like
a chance to prove to her what a successful teacher she
was.''

''Sounds like a super idea to me,'' he said affably.

Abbie shifted her feet, wishing he wouldn't be so quick
to accept something she viewed as a potential problem.
''Will your father be there?'' she asked, having second
thoughts.

''Yes, he usually stays around the house in the early
evening to get ready for the next day's sermon.''

''In that case, perhaps I'll take you up on your invitation,
Tricia. It might just be the perfect time to talk to him about
the wedding ceremony.''

''The wedding ceremony?'' Tricia echoed, her hopeful
smile fading. She had no idea things were moving this fast.

''I'd really like your father to marry Jamie and me.''

''Oh, sure . . . when?''

''Next Tuesday.''

''Tuesday?'' she all but squeaked. ''That's only four
days away.''

''I realize I'm not giving him much notice, but I also
remember that Tuesday evenings are generally free ones
for him. He can announce the wedding at church on Sunday
and invite the elders and their wives to witness the
ceremony.''

''Oh,'' she said again, her hopes plummeting.

''Are you okay, Tricia?''

She nodded. ''It's just that this is all so sudden.''

''It might seem so to you, lass,'' Jamie spoke up. ''But
I've had my eye on Abigail for some time now. I thought

Yesterday's Dream

we should be enjoying some married life here before returning to the jungle to complete my year out at the clinic.''

"If you'd rather forget about the dinner," Abbie suggested, "I'll understand."

"Oh no, it's still on." Her mind raced ahead, upping the time. "Is three o'clock suitable?"

"Jamie?" Abbie queried, looking up at him. He nodded. "Whatever you girls decide is fine with me."

"Then three o'clock it is."

"Good." Tricia turned to leave, then turned back again, looking unsure. Abbie encouraged her. "What is it?"

"If I stop by Saturday morning, do you think you could do something about my hair? Daddy's been getting on my case about it. Says no one will hire a girl who looks like she's inviting a mouse to take up residence in her hair. Only he didn't say it quite so delicately."

Abbie laughed. "Okay. Stop in around nine and I'll see what I can do."

In less than a half hour, Tricia was driving David's car up into the hills, her mind racing as she plotted. She was still planning on a workable scenario when she pulled behind the Mountain View Cafe to the twelve-unit motel. It had been an up-to-the-minute establishment when it was built in the fifties, but now it had the unkempt appearance of being many years from its heyday. In the dusty office, Tricia inquired which room was Miss Bartlett's, but the matronly clerk didn't want to give out that information until Tricia mentioned she was David Rossi's sister. The name rang a bell.

"Oh yes, Miss Bartlett did tell me about him. He was an old boyfriend she saw in the lounge the other night. As I understand, he even sang a song or two with her. The patrons loved the impromptu reunion of the Bartlett Pair."

"That's right. She invited David to her room after the

show, but he couldn't make it. Now I'd like to invite her over to the house, so could you tell me her unit number?''

"It's number seven," she offered without further prompting. "Says it's her lucky number. Better hurry, though, if you want to catch her. She'll soon be getting ready to do her show.''

After thanking the woman, Tricia left the small, musty-smelling office and walked down the low awning-covered porch that ran the length of the dozen rooms. She stopped before the red paint-chipped door with a brass number 7 on it and heard taped music playing from inside. Good, she was still there, Tricia thought. The teenager crossed her fingers, closed her eyes, and offered a quick prayer for success. Then she knocked solidly.

Patricia heard the advancing footsteps before the door squeaked open, and she found herself looking into the heavily made-up face of the country singer. This was the woman David was once romantically linked with? She looked so much older than the woman on the videotape.

"Yes, what is it?" the singer queried impatiently. "If you're selling something, I'm not interested."

Tricia gulped and quickly placed her hand out to stop the door from closing on her. "No, I'm not, but I do have an offer to make you.''

"Sorry, honey, but I'm really not interested," she almost shouted over the loud music. "I've got a show to do. Goodbye.''

"It concerns my brother, David Rossi," she said to the closed door.

A moment passed, then two. Tricia heard the music shut off. Then the door creaked open once again, and this time Tricia faced a smiling entertainer. "Why didn't you say that in the first place?''

"I tried to, but you seemed pretty determined not to give

Yesterday's Dream   129

me any of your time." Tricia responded as she stepped inside, moving forward to Becki's gesture.

The red and white bedspread was disheveled, bearing evidence of a recent nap, while her cowgirl boots lay on the carpet below. Becki walked to the green vinyl desk chair, pulled it out, and sat down. Then, nodding for her to do the same, Tricia moved one from the wall, its seat torn and covered with a wide strip of clear plastic tape.

"What's your first name, honey?"

Tricia paused, not sure if she was glad or not that David hadn't volunteered any information about her. If they were really close, wouldn't he have? She sat down. "Patricia, but I prefer to be called Tricia."

"My given name is Rebecca, though I like Becki, spelled with an i, better. Becki Bartlett. It's got a ring to it, don't you think." She crossed her leg and the fringes on the hem of her dress cascaded over it. Leaning forward, she continued, "I have fifteen minutes till show time, so let's get right down to business. Why are you here, Tricia?"

Chapter Nine

"Tricia, what in the world is all the fuss about? Why are you so insistent that I get dressed in a sports coat and tie. And what's this with your new hairdo?"

"Daddy hated the way I was wearing my hair, so I thought I would show him I could be a compliant daughter and wear a more traditional style. Is it an improvement?" she asked as she stroked her hair. Patricia neglected to tell him she hadn't been to a professional beautician, but to the Kenans. Abbie, under her mother's tutelage, had suggested they cut the frizzle away and do her hair in a style similar to Abigail's.

"Yes, it's a big improvement," David agreed. "The outfit's good too. I like to see women in long dresses—they look soft and feminine. I don't know whom to thank, but your taste in the world of fashion has vastly improved since you've returned."

That too is credited to Abbie, she wanted to admit but didn't. Tricia hadn't worn the black floral dress until that day. "I wanted to do something special for Daddy. He's been the keynote speaker at that regional conference, and I just thought it would be sort of neat to surprise him, let

130

Yesterday's Dream 131

him know I appreciate him. That we appreciate him," Tricia clarified, hoping she sounded convincing as she opened the oven door to check on the roast.

David's face softened. "You keep that up, he's not going to want you to leave . . . ever. You're special, Patricia Rossi, and had I tried, I couldn't have picked a kinder, more caring girl to be my sister."

Closing the oven door, Tricia braved a smile, feeling more than a little guilty. It wasn't her father she was doing this for, but for David. Please, she silently prayed, don't let my plans go awry.

"Anything I can do to help?"

"You could light the candelabrum and sit it on the table."

"Candlelight? Tricia, isn't that a tad bit romantic for a Dad-appreciation dinner?"

"No," she said with an innocent shrug. "It'll add to the atmosphere of the meal."

"Yeah," he said, snatching the matches from off the shelf. "In case you mess it up, it won't be as noticeable as it would under the glare of the ceiling light."

Tricia playfully bopped him on the top of the head with her oven mitt. "This is also an appreciation-brother-meal. And I'd better not blow it when I'm trying so darn hard."

"If the meat's tough and the potatoes are dry, we'll forgive you. You know how that old saying goes about the thought." David finished by leaning forward to give her a kiss on the cheek.

Patricia watched with a mixture of feelings as he went to the closet and lifted down the silver candelabrum from off the top shelf. Then he turned to the table and for the first time really noticed it. His dark brows knit as his worried eyes lifted to meet hers. "Hey, there's six places set here."

"Um-hum," she hummed nonchalantly. "I invited a couple of dinner guests."

"Like who?" David queried, immediately suspicious.

"It's a surprise."

"Candlelight . . . fancy dress . . . new hairdo . . ." David's voice rose as he counted each off on his fingers. "Patricia, you haven't invited the Kenans and that doctor over, have you?"

"Now, David, calm down," she said, moving around the table as he circled after her.

"Have you?" he dogged. "Have you invited Maggie, Abigail, and that doctor over for our special dinner?"

"Well . . . yes and no."

He stopped. "What kind of an answer is that? Are you trying to tell me they invited themselves over?"

"No."

"Well then?" he spread his hands in an imploring gesture.

"I invited them, yes. But not all that you mentioned," she admitted in a small voice.

"Oh? Which of them didn't you invite and it had better be the doctor."

"Please, David, he does have a name, you know."

"Tricia!" His face turned red with suppressed anger, wondering where was this girl's mind after all he had told her. "How could you! How could you invite them over knowing—"

The doorbell cut his words short. She gulped. "Will you please get that?"

"Yeah, I'll get it on my way out. You can entertain those two by yourself, Miss Benedict Arnold!"

"David, please, you can't leave like this," she pleaded, hurrying right behind him. "And don't say anything to Abigail in a fit of anger that will later come back to haunt you."

Yesterday's Dream   133

But when he swung the door open, it was to face a bubbling Rebecca Bartlett on the front porch. "Davie!" she squealed, the first to speak. "Don't you all look spiffy and polished tonight." She looked past his shoulder to Patricia and cupped her hand in a girlish wave. "Hello, Tricia."

"Hi, Becki." Patricia returned her grin but felt she looked stiff and unnatural. She would have been deaf not to have heard the tail end of their sibling shouting match.

Snapping his gaping mouth shut, David looked mutely from one to the other for a moment. "You know each other?"

"Sure we do. Tricia came to visit me yesterday at the Mountain View and invited me for dinner."

"Oh did she now? But how did she know where to find . . ." Then it hit him. The video and the heart-to-heart conversation that followed. He turned to his sister and smiled tightly. The little conniver! His expression seemed to convey, just wait until I get you alone.

"Davie," Becki said again, this time some of the joy going out of her eyes. "Didn't you know I was coming? I mean, you're all dressed up. I thought it was your idea that I come for dinner." The hurt oozed from her pouting lips.

David forced an apologetic smile and was about to admit he hadn't the foggiest notion that she was coming when his attention was diverted. Abbie's car was pulling up the drive with her Scotsman sitting beside her just as big as you please. Rearranging his expression, he drew in a deep breath and turned to an unsure Rebecca. His smile broadened as he offered his arm. "Becki, I'm thrilled to death you could make it tonight. Dinner's ready if you are."

Rebecca entered, her dimples prominent as she greedily took his arm and clutched it. Then she glanced over her shoulder to the pair getting out of the car. "Oh, no! Is that what's-her-name?"

"Abigail Kenan? Yes, I'm afraid it is. But don't fret, she and Crocodile Dundee are Tricia's guests, not mine."

"Who? You mean Abigail's dating that Australian movie star?"

"Hardly! It's Doctor Jamie MacIlhaney," he explained with an edge of jealousy in his tone. "He lives in the Brazilian jungle amidst headhunters and guerrillas."

"He what?" Becki turned, her arm still tucked tightly into David's. She watched the advancing couple, first looking horrified, then fascinated. "Well, well, this should be an interesting evening after all," she said. And when they got to the door, she ignored Abbie and thrust her hand out to the man in the khaki safari shirt. "Hello, Doctor Mackel. I'm Rebecca Bartlett, but my friends call me Becki."

"Good evening, Becki, but that's MacIlhaney," he said, good-naturedly, clasping her hand in his.

"So, you live in the jungle. A real life Tarzan."

Abbie rolled her eyes, then turned her attention to David. "And a good evening to you, David. I didn't realize you were going to be here."

"I assure you, that assumption was mutual. It appears my little sister neglected to inform either of us just who was on her guest list . . . did you?" he finished with a challenge, looking her square in the eye.

Tricia evaded his question. "Dinner's ready," she announced with a hopeful smile. "Follow me, please."

The foursome trailed behind Patricia and found Bill standing at the table, nibbling on a carrot stick. His eyes fell on Becki and his jaws froze in mid-chew as she wiggled by in a champagne-color dress, a size too small.

"I don't believe I know this young lady, David," he said with a forced smile beneath a disapproving brow.

"Rebecca Bartlett."

"But all her friends call her Becki," Abbie couldn't help but add. "She was the lead singer for the Bartlett Pair."

Yesterday's Dream   135

"Bartlett Pair?" Bill's frown creased deeper. "Wasn't that the duo David once belonged to?"

"That's right." Becki extended her hand to him. "Davie tells me you're a man of the cloth."

He nodded, shooting his son a look of bewilderment as he shook her hand.

"Davie told me a lot about you and Mrs. Rossi when we were doing our gigs together several years back. I feel I know you already."

"Unfortunately, I can't say the feeling's mutual. I didn't realize you were back in his life."

"Thanks to a chance meeting, though I've never forgotten him. We made beautiful music together. We still do, at least that's what folks tell me after we sang a duet at the club the other night."

"You sang a song together at the club?" Bill repeated, his heart sinking as he felt he was losing control over his children once again.

The chair legs scraped along the tile as they seated themselves. Becki was the only one who was unaware of the tension at the table. She glanced around. "Where is she?"

"To whom are you referring, Miss Bartlett?" Bill asked as he pressed the glass of ice water against his flushed cheek. He wasn't sure yet which of his children were responsible for this fiasco, but when he found out, there had better be a good explanation.

"Mrs. Rossi, of course," she said innocently as she draped her napkin over her skirt.

"There is no Mrs. Rossi," he said with controlled patience.

That was the first moment that Becki was aware of the strained emotions of those seated around the table. Looking at the solemn faces, she came to the wrong conclusion. "Oh, Reverend, I am sorry. I wasn't aware that your wife passed away." Then she looked at David with an accusing eye. "Shame on you, Davie, you should have told me. Here I am, going on about your poor dead mother."

Silence. Total silence. Then Tricia stepped forward and sat the dish of roast beef on the table. This was not a good idea. Her hands shook as she pulled her own chair out, but somehow she managed to keep her voice steady when she asked her red-faced father to give the blessing on the food.

"Do you encounter many dangerous animals living in the jungle, doctor?" Becki asked as she watched him lift another slice of meat onto his plate.

Jamie glanced up, glad for a safe topic. "Oh yes, lass. We have anacondas. They grow up to twenty-six feet in length, you know, which makes them the longest snake in the Western Hemisphere. They're actually capable of swallowing a deer whole. But to be truthful, more river folks fear the bushmaster and the somewhat smaller fer-de-lance. They're guided to their prey by the victim's body heat."

"Ooh," Becki shivered, hugging her arms. "You must be brave to live in such a place."

"Or crazy," David said, taking a fork full of potatoes.

Jamie bristled. "Excuse me?"

"That's David's weak attempt at being funny," Abbie said with a lightness she didn't really feel. Then she gave him a challenging look across the table. "Isn't it?"

"No," he replied, refusing to back down. His eyes met hers and held. "The jungle's no place for a woman. She might get hurt," he said, diverting his attention back to Jamie now.

"Abigail could get hurt here too," he pointed out, jabbing his fork in his mound of green beans. "Anyway, we try to take precautions to keep mishaps to a minimum." But sometimes even that isn't good enough, he thought, briefly seeing Delores in his mind's eye. He pushed his

Yesterday's Dream

dead fiancee from his thoughts as he gave Abbie an adoring smile, which she returned.

David noticed and shifted uncomfortably in his chair. "Well, at least she won't be going back."

"Oh, but she will—for a year while I finish my term at the clinic."

"She'd be more comfortable here."

"Unquestionably, but I prefer to have my wife at my side."

"Your wife," David repeated, and it hit him with no less force than it had when he heard this dream-wrecker refer to Abbie in that context at the school.

Jamie reached over and clasped Abbie's hand before continuing. "That's one of the reasons I agreed to come along tonight. I wanted to speak to the Reverend about marrying us on Tuesday in the parlor of Chestnut Hill."

The fork slipped from David's hand, clinking the china and shooting a bean onto the white linen tablecloth. Becki nervously giggled at his awkwardness, breaking the tension-filled moment as she slipped her arm through his. "I think that's so romantic."

"Romantic?" David spat out. "It's crazy! Just plain crazy!"

"Will you quit saying that, David," Abbie snapped. "It may not be the way you'd do things, but it's how I want to do them. The parlor will be a beautiful setting for a wedding ceremony, and I will be the third generation of Kenan women to be married there."

"Darn it all, Abbie! You don't go around marrying someone out of gratitude."

"Abigail is not marrying me out of gratitude," Jamie countered, his cheeks uncharacteristically rosy.

"Sure she is. You saved her from those guerrillas and now she wants to pay you back by marrying you."

138   *JoAnn Sands*

"You saved her from the gorillas?" Becki squealed. "I
thought they were only found in Africa."

"Men, Rebecca," David snapped, losing patience with
them all. "We're talking about men here."

"Actually, we're talking about a wedding ceremony,"
Jamie said. "Well, Reverend, what do you say? Will you
be free to marry us on Tuesday evening?"

"He can't," Tricia spoke up, unable to keep silent a
moment longer. "He's got visitation."

"So do it during the day," Becki said, liking the idea
of marrying off her competition, and the sooner the better.

"No, he can't," David stated.

"Why not?" Jamie asked.

David's mind raced. He couldn't think of a valid reason,
at least not one he could say out loud. But Tricia could and
did. "Because Abbie's in love with my brother."

"Patricia!" Abbie gasped.

"Yes you are!" Tricia insisted. "You two are meant for
each other. Why is it I'm the only one willing to admit
that?"

Abbie's tight smile was without humor. "It's all beginning to make sense now. The real reason for this dinner
isn't a reward of sorts, for me giving you cooking lessons,
but rather to make me jealous of Rebecca's attention to
David and thereby come to my senses. Aren't I right?"

Tricia hesitated a moment, then nodded reluctantly,
though a stubborn hope remained in her eyes. "Okay, I
admit it. You're right. Is there a chance that my well-
intended plan just might work after all?"

"Not a prayer! Patti, of all the juvenile stunts you've
pulled, this has got to be the dumbest!" David yelled, shov-
ing his plate away. It clipped the side of his saucer, spilling
his untouched coffee over its side.

"You don't have to sound so belligerent, David. I'm
only trying to help you," she half scolded, reaching over

Yesterday's Dream

to try to wipe up the growing stain on Sheila's good linen tablecloth. She retrieved the lone bean too and placed it on her own saucer.

"Help me? You've caused a scene here!"

"If there's a scene, it's you who's escalating it. Let me point out, it's not me who's doing all the yelling."

"Oh? So this fiasco is all my fault. You told me this was a dinner to honor Dad."

"David . . . Patricia, that's enough." Bill spoke in a quiet, though commanding tone. "If you two can't speak civilly to each other, then don't converse."

David raked a nervous hand through his hair. Never had he and Patti had such hot words, and to have them exchanged in front of Abbie and that . . . that intruder was all the more humiliating. His eyes met the couple and held. Jamie's arm was sliding around Abbie's shoulder in an obvious effort to comfort her. Well, two could play that game. He put his arm around Becki, which in turn encouraged her to lean closer to him.

"You don't love your 'Jungle Jim,' " David insisted, refusing to back down from a stare that was making her uncomfortable. He could tell, she was fidgeting with her napkin. She always fidgeted with something when she was uneasy.

The fidgeting stopped, her small fist knotted, and she tilted her chin in an air of defiance. "I care more about Jamie than you ever cared for your country-crooning girl-friend. If you loved her, you would have married her years ago when you were the other half of the Bartlett Pair." She broke into a nervous chuckle. "Honestly, that name is so . . ." she broke off

"So what, Abbie?" David pressed.

"Corny." She shrugged. "I mean, you can't possibly expect to be taken seriously."

"Oh? Well let me tell you something, Abigail. The folks

loved us at the club the other night. We had them in the palm of our hand and that felt good. A natural high. Becki,'' he said, turning to her, ''will you marry me?''

Tricia's eyes grew large with shock. This wasn't supposed to happen! Her brother was to declare his love for Abbie, not to this . . . this floozie, who now had her arms entwined around David's neck, saying, yes . . . yes . . . yes! and smothering his flushed cheek with kisses.

Abbie caught her breath in sheer dismay. What had she done? Gloated and dared him into doing something he would never have on his own? She couldn't picture him binding himself to this crass, shaggy-haired woman for a year, to say nothing of a lifetime. They were as wrong for each other as Bill and Sheila had been. And look what their ill-fated love had gotten them. The only good thing that came of their union had been David. She counted to ten, hoping to rein in her rising temper.

Meanwhile, David disengaged himself from Becki's clinging grasp. His own laughter had a hollow ring to it. ''You never were one for hiding your enthusiasm when you were happy.''

Bill wasn't laughing, but watched the scene being played out before him beneath a deepening frown of disapproval. ''Aren't you behaving a bit rashly, David? I don't find upstaging Abigail and Jamie very amusing.''

''Tit for tat? Is that what you're thinking?'' Locking his hands behind his head, he took a deep breath and tried to look assertive. He didn't quite succeed. ''For your information, Dad, I nearly did marry Becki once. We got to know each other well during our gigs in Tennessee.''

''Your gigs?''

''Yeah. We'd take a job for a specific time at these clubs. You know,'' he explained with a nonchalant shrug.

''Yes, I'm afraid I do. In that case, son, I suppose you'd better get married and make an honest woman of her.''

Yesterday's Dream

"Daddy!" Patricia squealed. The last thing she wanted was for him to give his blessing to them, though he was scarcely doing that.

"Patti, please." He held up his hand in a gesture to silence her. "You've done quite enough for one evening. I assume this dinner was all your idea."

Patricia's lips quivered, and without another word, she hurried from the room, bursting into tears.

There was a heavy silence among the five, who stared at one another for a few moments. Then Jamie spoke. "Reverend, I don't mean to keep pressing the issue, but will you be free to marry Abigail and me on Tuesday evening? If you would rather not, we could find someone who will . . . a J.P. if nothing else."

Bill's eyes shifted to the woman who sat rather forlorn and stiff beside Jamie. She looked as befuddled as he felt, not the picture of the anxious bride-to-be. "Abigail, is this what you want?" he asked, his tone suddenly punctuated with concern.

"You're my minister," Abbie reminded him as her eyes lifted to meet his. "I always thought that when the time came, you would be the one to perform the ceremony."

Nodding in resignation, he reached in his pocket for a notepad and ballpoint pen. "We have to discuss such matters as selected readings, music, witnesses, etc." He clicked the pen point down and hovered it over the paper. "So, let's get started, shall we."

David took Becki by the hand and coaxed her to her feet. "Come on, we'd better let these two lovebirds discuss their wedding in private. Besides, we have plans of our own to make."

Abbie looked at him with a breaking heart. Don't do this . . . don't do this to spite me, she wanted to cry out. Haven't you learned anything from your past? Instead, she forced a smile, clasping Jamie's hand in a grip which caused him to look curiously at her. "Good night, David."

His eyes met hers and it seemed he looked down to the very depths of her soul. "Goodbye, Abigail."

Chapter Ten

When Bill Rossi gave his sermon the following morning, he managed to keep his feelings in check and his thoughts focused on the lesson he'd prepared. Now, as he greeted his congregation in the vestibule of the church, he felt a bit out of touch and his mind kept drifting back to last night. He wanted to dislike Jamie MacIlhaney, but he couldn't. He was a personable young man, one who obviously cared deeply for Abigail. Ironic, how both mother and daughter rejected father and son, although in all fairness, he wasn't even sure if Margaret understood the depth of his feelings for her. Did she even suspect that her sudden marriage to Jeremy Kenan had caused him to chose such an unsuitable wife?

One by one, the members of his congregation shook his hand while complimenting him on his sermon. One of those was Jamie. His smile was broad and sincere, apparently feeling no ill will over the rocky beginnings of their evening together last night. Informal as ever, he was tieless and dressed in the same short-sleeved khaki shirt he wore last night. Then there was Abbie, who didn't look quite as relaxed. Bill had announced their upcoming marriage and

143

invited the elders and their wives to witness their very private ceremony in the Kenan parlor at seven on Tuesday evening. As he shook her soft, slender hand, he was reminded anew that he had never quite put it from his mind that this young woman could one day be his daughter-in-law. But in fifty-six hours, more or less, that wishful thinking would end. At that appointed hour, it would be he who would be joining the hands of Abigail and Jamie Mac-Ilhaney in holy matrimony. They exchanged brief pleasantries before he turned to the next in line—a little boy with a healthy crop of red hair, bangs down over his forehead, and freckles splattered across his nose and pudgy cheeks.

"Good morning, Kevin," he said, bending forward to shake the child's hand.

"Good morning, preacher. That sure was a neat story about Samson fighting the lion."

"Yes, he certainly was brave to do that. Perhaps you'll grow up to be brave too."

His grin grew even broader. "I hope so. Jamie's brave. He saved Miss Abigail from some gorillas. Did you hear about that?"

"Kevin," Abbie said, overhearing the conversation and turned around to admonish him. "How many times have we explained to you it wasn't that kind of a gorilla. They were men—bad men."

"I know that," he admitted. "But it sounds neater if folks think it's the other kind."

Bill threw back his head and laughed. "Man or beast, it was a brave thing Doctor Mac did." He ruffled the boy's hair with his hand, liking his enthusiasm. "You come back and see us again, son." Then he turned to Margaret, who followed the trio. The touch of her hand in his stirred something within and he held it a moment or two longer than necessary. "Good morning, Maggie."

Yesterday's Dream

"Reverend." She returned his smile, but not his informality. "Good sermon as always. Samson's an engaging character, though he brought his father a ton of grief when he took up with that Philistine woman."

Bill nodded, his smile fading as he mused for a moment, that there was something in the story that each age group could identify with and grasp. Even he, unfortunately. "Children don't always follow in the way their parents want," he said with a telling sigh.

Did she know about Rebecca, he wondered? Abbie would have told her. Still, she gave no hint that she knew and was simply referring to the Israelite judge who'd lived so long ago. As a matter of fact, her smile and direct look into his eyes told him she hadn't. Her cool hand slipped from his and she moved on. A fleeting fantasy entered his mind. What would it be like to have this tall blonde, always impeccable in dress and manners, standing next to him, greeting others with her warm handshake. Sheila had always complained about this one whose handshake was too limp and insincere or that one which was too forceful and made her wince in pain.

"Reverend Rossi, good sermon."

Tearing his gaze from Maggie's back, he began to smile to the little white-haired lady with a worn straw hat. "Someone should take up a collection to buy her a new one," Sheila had said cattily on more than one occasion. Bill smiled, genuinely liking this woman. "Thank you, Grace. And congratulations on the birth of your new grandson. Let's see now . . . this is number seven?"

After the last of the congregation had filed out, Bill turned his attention to the lone figure still there. Patricia was bending over to retrieve a piece of lint from the carpet and removed a discarded bulletin from a straightback vestibule chair. She always liked to see the sanctuary in perfect order. He could still visualize her in the Sunday School rooms, straightening the little wooden chairs and gathering up stray crayons, while she waited patiently for him to take her to her new home.

Bill spoke her name and she turned. "Yes, Daddy?"

She looks so sad, he thought. They had virtually swept last night's disastrous get-together under the rug and hadn't come to terms with what had happened. He knew she was hurting as much as he. Bill couldn't lose her as he'd lost Sheila and was now in the process of losing David. He would do all within his power not to, and he had a plan. It had taken root in his mind as he lay in bed last night, and how he would act upon his thought.

"Patti . . . um. . . . Tricia," he corrected in an effort to please her. "Last evening wasn't entirely your fault, you know. You meant well, but you forgot, David has a free will and he doesn't happen to view Rebecca quite the way you and I do."

"She's a modern-day Delilah."

Bill grunted. "I couldn't agree with you more. But your brother's a man now and is capable of making his own decisions when it comes to matters of the heart."

"I'm not so sure about that." She tossed up her hands in despair. "Had only I not tried to play matchmaker! Me and my bright ideas. I wanted to make them jealous and and long for the 'good old days' when they were the sweethearts of Laurel Springs High. But I had to push it to a head because Abbie was about to marry her jungle doctor."

"And still is."

Tricia nodded glumly. "And even worse, David's decided to make that country-crooning-creature his wife. Sometimes I wish the ground would just open up and swallow me."

"Now, Tricia, you don't mean that."

"Yes I do. Everything I try fails miserably."

Yesterday's Dream　　　　147

"That's simply not true. Maybe you didn't achieve the desired result, but the dinner you prepared couldn't have been tastier."

"Really?" she asked, lifting a critical brow.

"Really. In just a couple weeks of practice, you're a better cook than Sheila was in her twenty-three years as a housewife. I'm proud of you."

"You are?"

"Why must you question everything I say?"

"Because I let you down constantly. I've been trying to find a job but with little success. About the only place I haven't tried is the Mountain View Cafe."

"I have a much better idea. I need a secretary. Here all along, there's the perfect choice sleeping under my roof only it didn't hit me until last night."

"Oh, Daddy," Tricia said, with a sad wag of her head. "You don't have to offer me a job because you feel sorry for me."

"I'm not. I'm offering you the job of church secretary because I badly need one. You know how busy I am. I've been spreading myself too thin for too many months now. It would help me a lot."

"What would you want me to do?" she asked, the idea beginning to sound more agreeable now that she felt he wasn't offering the position out of pity.

Bill began to enumerate. "Answer the phone. You've got a very appealing speaking voice, you know. You'd set up appointments for counseling and visitation. You would also be expected to send out letters on matters pertaining to business and activities of the church. We need bulletins made up each Sunday and programs for special events. As we're using the computer more and more, I'll show you how to familiarize yourself with it. Our budget isn't the biggest, but I can afford to pay more than minimum wage.

148   *JoAnn Sands*

What do you say, Tricia? Does it sound like something you might want to explore further?''

''Oh yes, Daddy, yes! It sounds so much better than the factory or the cafe.''

''Well, here at least you won't be hassled or harrassed.''

He joined in on her laughter, then sobered as he flicked off the foyer lights and opened the door. If only David's problem could be handled as easily. If he were really serious about this Bartlett woman, would he even want to remain at the school? Or would he tear off chasing after yesterday's dream? At this point, Bill just wasn't sure. David seemed to have inherited a streak of his mother's wild nature . . . her lust for living life on the edge. He could give him advice, if he would take it. Other than that he could only stand back and watch his son destroy himself with the wrong kind of woman—just as Samson of old had. And that thought about broke his heart.

''Will you please see that Mrs. Kenan gets her roasting pan back, Ruby,'' Bill Rossi said as he stood on the front porch. ''My daughter borrowed it and forgot to return it after church this morning. I wasn't sure if you'd be needing it today or not.''

''You didn't have to make a special trip, Reverend. I've got scads of cookware.''

''Who is it, Rube?'' Maggie asked, entering the hallway. She recognized Bill's sun-silhouetted form and she smiled. ''Hello, Bill, come on in.''

He didn't want to; he simply wanted to hand the pan back and leave, but his legs seemed to have a mind of their own and he found himself crossing over the threshold of the Kenan plantation-style home. And once inside, he handed the pan to Ruby, who, smiling in an unsettling conspiratorial way, turned and walked out, leaving them by themselves.

Yesterday's Dream   149

"I missed seeing your son in the service this morning, Bill."

Of all the things she could have said, that was the very last topic he wanted to touch on. Maggie had unknowingly pressed his "hot button." Less than thirty minutes ago, he and David had had an argument, and with his feelings still hurt and his temper elevated, he should never have come to the Kenan house. He hadn't heeded to common sense, and he was more aware of that by the second. He clenched his jaw for a moment, then began to speak in a controlled manner. "With all that must be on your mind these days, Maragret, I'm surprised you've taken notice of that."

She arched her brow. Was there a barb in his tone or was she just imagining it? Nonetheless she smiled. "I'm aware of what's going on around me."

"Are you?"

Now that smile faded. So, she hadn't imagined that verbal jab. Maggie crossed her arms. "What's that supposed to mean?"

"Must I spell it out? My son wasn't in the service this morning because your daughter has hurt him deeply. He's in love with her, and I don't think there's ever been a time when he hasn't been."

"Bill," she said in an injured tone. "I'm sorry he's hurt; I truly am. But my daughter's in love with Jamie. I thought you approved or you wouldn't be officiating at the ceremony."

"How can I approve when her decision is causing David to suffer? Yet how can I refuse her request when she's not only a member of the congregation but the church has been supporting her work in Brazil as well. I'm caught between that proverbial rock and a hard place with no wiggle room to spare."

"Bill, I . . . I don't know what to say."

Kevin entered the room at that point. "Hi, preacher."

He grinned, unaware of the stress between the two adults. "I caught a frog out in the pond. Wanna see 'im?"

Bill's somber expression softened as he looked down at the likeable little boy. But Maggie's brows knit. "Where is it?"

"Here," he said, extracting the frog from the pocket of his light denim jacket.

The woman gasped. "Oh, Kev! Get rid of that thing," she ordered, unable to bring herself to take it from him.

"What do I do with him?"

"Take it outside."

"But I wanna keep him. I need a pet."

"You've got Shadow."

"He's your dog," Kevin pointed out.

"Maybe so, but as long as you're here, consider him yours as well. However, while you're living under my roof, I will not allow nature's slimy critters to share it with you."

"Frankie's not slimy."

"You've given him a name?" Maggie rolled her eyes, then pointed to the door. "Take him out. Now."

Bill smiled in spite of the situation. How like David he was when he was that age. Always bringing a menagerie of animals into the house, also much to Sheila's dismay. "Better listen to Maggie, young man. A house is no place for a frog. They prefer the outdoors."

"Oh, all right." He opened the door just as Marcella Wells had lifted her finger to press the bell. Startled, Kevin loosened his grip on the frog and it hopped out of his small hand and landed on the social worker's sandaled foot.

She screamed.

Kevin grinned, childishly glad to have frightened her, but not happy to see the woman. His smile soon vanished though, and ended in a scowl. "What do you want?"

Her hand went to her racing heart as her eyes searched the porch, but the amphibian had already disappeared. She

Yesterday's Dream 151

lifted her gaze then to the boy, and her mouth twisted in restrained anger. "You did that on purpose."

"Did not. You scared us and it jumped."

"He didn't mean to frighten you, ma'am," Bill said, placing a light hand on the boy's shoulder, warning him by his gesture to say nothing more. Then he presented his polished, professional smile, seeing the question in her eyes and wanting to disarm her hostility. "I'm William Rossi, a friend of the family."

"Marcella Wells, Child Welfare," she said, offering neither her hand or her smile.

"What brings you here, Miss Wells?"

"I wanted to see for myself just how Kevin was coming along."

"On a Sunday?" he queried, but Kevin spoke up. "I'm doin' fine. I like it here," he continued, pressing against Bill, whom he decided was an ally.

"I'm sure you do." Her eyes lifted to meet Maggie's and the younger woman could distinguish a faint glimmer there. "I think we might have found a couple to take Kevin off your hands."

"Who?" Maggie asked, her back stiffening. The thought saddened her more than she'd expected.

"A couple from Asheville. They own a photography business and would like to take in a child. They have none of their own."

Kevin looked up at his temporary caregiver, suddenly feeling very contrite. "Please, Miss Margaret, can't I stay here with you and . . . and the preacher. I won't bring any more frogs into the house. I promise."

Maggie shifted her feet uncomfortably. "Honey, you knew when Abbie brought you here, it was only going to be for a short time, until other, more permanent plans could be made."

"But . . . but you got such a big house. And you don't got your own little boy any more."

"I'll tell you something else I don't have any more, and that's a husband."

His little chin quivered. "I won't go away with her and live with some stranger. If you don't want me, then maybe I'll run away with Abbie and Doctor Mac. They do like me and in a couple of days they'll be married."

"Kevin, be reasonable," Maggie pleaded. "You can't go running off to the jungle, even if it were legally possible. You can't live like that."

"Folks would have said I couldn't hide away in the school for several weeks either, but I did, didn't I!" And with that shouted in frustration, he turned and disappeared back inside the house, slamming the door behind him.

Maggie drew in a deep breath before turning to Marcella. "I apologize for the boy's behavior, but in all truth, I can understand how he must feel."

"The department knows what's best for the child, and a married couple, where one of them can always be around to care for him, is what's best."

"He's not left alone here," Maggie assured her. "When I'm working, Ruby and her husband are around to see that he has proper supervision and stays out of trouble."

"I see. Apparently someone slipped up today when he tossed that slimy frog at me."

"The frog wasn't slimy, and he didn't toss it at you. You startled him and it jumped."

"If you insist," she said, bored with it all. "I'll let you know just as soon as the couple's ready. They wanted to get the guest room papered and painted first. Seeing your fondness for the boy, I'm sure you won't mind keeping him a few more days."

She turned to leave and Bill spoke up. "Miss Wells, I find it highly irregular for a social worker to be dropping

Yesterday's Dream   153

by this day. Do you usually work on a Sunday?'' Finally he asked the question she'd yet to answer, now that she wasn't distracted by Kevin.

Marcella shook her head. ''No. I was shopping at the new mall and it happens I pass your place on my way home. So I decided to stop and save myself the intended visit tomorrow. Good day.''

Margaret watched until the woman got back into her minivan and drove away. Bill saw the longing on her face as her eyes followed her down the road until she was out of sight. ''You really like that boy, don't you Maggie?''

She nodded, but with some reluctance. ''At first I fought it.'' Her face softened. ''He reminds me so much of Jerry. As it turned out, it's a good thing I kept his toys and clothing.''

''A good thing? Maggie, you've been no more able to let go of Jerry and his possessions than you have been his father's.''

''You're wrong about that, Bill. I've given Jamie Jeremy's clothing and medical equipment, and, I hope, his hometown practice when his work in Brazil is over next year.''

''Where the memory of Doctor Kenan can live on in the next generation.''

''Bill, Bill,'' Maggie said, shaking her head in dismay. ''First you attack my daughter and now my husband. Who's next, me?''

''I'm sorry. I don't want to hurt you, as I'm sure Abbie didn't want to hurt my son. But the fact is, we are hurt . . . father and son hurt by the Kenan women, though it be a generation apart. Oh, Maggie,'' he sighed, running a frustrated hand through his hair. She appeared startled by both his statement and action. ''You say you're aware of what's going on around you? Then why don't you notice that I long for you. Remember when we played Spin-the-Bottle

154 *JoAnn Sands*

at Tommy's birthday party? I actually prayed it would stop at you and that prayer was answered.''

"Bill, we were children. And if my mother had realized I was kissing you three times . . .''

"Four."

She shrugged, feeling uncomfortable. "Who was keeping count?'

"I was. I told Tommy that night, when I grew up I was going to marry you.''

"Reverend, it appears you were wrong on that score. And I bet you're going to feel awfully silly tomorrow after making this confession this afternoon,'' she chided with a smile.

"Maybe, but it's got to be said. I waited too long. I wanted to ask you out but I was too shy, and when I finally gathered the courage, Jeremy had walked into your life. I couldn't compete with a suitor-physician then any more than David can now. And the end result was and is, we go running into the arms of women who are so wrong for us, expecting to find comfort but finding heartache instead. I did it with Sheila and now it looks like David's doing it with Rebecca. We had an argument about that when he come home after being out all night, doing heaven only knows what. David, more than anyone, knows what marriage on the rebound can do. It ruined my private life and could have ruined my professional one as well, had my congregation not been so compassionate and understanding.''

There, he finally said what was on his heart and felt better for it . . . now, anyway. But Maggie looked astonished, as though it was a totally new revelation to her and she could only stare up at him in disbelief. Boldly, he reached out and touched her flushed cheek. "I'm not angry at you, Maggie. Please understand that. I can only hope that speaking what's been weighing so heavily on my mind will give me closure and a measure of peace of mind.''

Yesterday's Dream

He waited a moment for her to respond, and when she didn't, he turned and walked back to his car.

Five minutes later, Maggie was still standing on the porch, her arms folded, staring into space and pondering all he had said. When Abbie and Jamie pulled up the drive. When Abbie asked her what was wrong, she only shook her head and said they were just in time for some of Ruby's peach crumb pie.

Chapter Eleven

When Tricia opened the door early Tuesday evening, she found herself face-to-face with Becki Bartlett. She was wearing an attention-getting red satin dress. "Let me guess, you're here to see David," Tricia said dryly, still depressed over the dinner, which not only resulted in the wedding going on as planned, but with her brother proposing to this woman whom he really didn't love.

"He's escorting me to the wedding."

"I don't think he's going."

"Don't be silly; of course he's going. He told me so this morning when we talked on the phone."

At that point, Bill walked into the room, straightening his dark tie, when his eyes came to rest on the woman in the minidress. He nodded in recognition. " 'Evening, Rebecca."

The woman grinned at him, showing off her big dimples. "Reverend, I forgot to bring my umbrella, and it looks as though we might have ourselves a storm before the night's over. May I borrow one of yours?"

His eyes flickered to Tricia's. "I think Sheila left one behind in the closet. Would you look, please?"

156

Yesterday's Dream
157

Wordlessly, she opened the door, reached up to the shelf, and brought down a bright yellow umbrella. As she handed it to Becki, she commented, "It'll clash with your outfit and might cause some folks to stare."

"I'm used to it. I guess I have the type of face and body that people are prone to stare at."

Tricia rolled her eyes. Normally she would have quietly laughed behind a shielding hand at such a self-inflated opinion, but that day she was in no mood for laughing. It was one of the worst days of her life. She turned to her father and thought he looked more like he was going to a funeral than a wedding, with his dark suit and grim expression.

Their eyes met and held. "Are you ready to leave, Tricia?"

"Not quite, but you go. I'll come with David a little later. That is," she said facing Rebecca once again, "if you don't mind."

Becki shrugged. "Suit yourself."

"Keep an eye on the clock, honey," Bill advised. "It's distracting to everyone when you walk in late after the ceremony's already begun."

Tricia nodded mutely, watched him leave, then went into the kitchen, turned on the radio, and stared out the window at the thickening clouds. Becki was right. It was going to be a stormy night.

Becki walked down the hall, her silver sling-back high heels thumping on the striped runner until she came to a stop before David's door. She rapped lightly. "Davie?"

"Come in."

She swung the door open, and her expectant smile faded. He was sitting on an armless chair, his head in his hands, his bare feet showing beneath his jeans. A frown wrinkled her brow, and she stamped her foot impatiently. "David! You aren't even dressed yet!"

158   *JoAnn Sands*

He slowly lifted his head and looked at her with wounded eyes. "I'm not going. I thought I could, but I can't. I just can't."

"Why on earth not?"

"Becki," he said in an almost pleading tone. "Let's just let the matter drop, shall we? I'm sorry I couldn't reach you before you left the motel. I did call, but you'd already gone."

She entered the room now and stood over him with her hands on her hips. "You're still in love with her, aren't you? That's why you can't go and see your beloved get married. Aren't I right?"

He stared up at her, annoyed.

"Aren't I right?" she hounded, her tone rising.

"Yes! Yes, you're right." He got up and walked to the window and looked out at the wind-bobbing branches of the large pine. "I admit it. You satisfied?"

She followed him over to the window. "No. No, I am not satisfied. You need to watch that ceremony, David. You need to know, really know, that it is finally over between you two and that tonight, it will be his bed she shares and not yours."

David sucked in his breath and counted to ten as he watched the branches sway. When he finally spoke, his voice was calm and quiet. "Will you please leave, Rebecca. If you don't mind, I'd rather be alone."

"But I do mind," she said stubbornly, rooted at his side.

Turning his head, he looked into her eyes and saw anything but compassion there. He tried to explain it to her. "Last night at the cafe, I thought I could stand to watch her marry MacIlhaney, but now with my head clear, I know I can't do that. I can't witness her being given to another man. And my own father, I feel, is a traitor to marry them. Now, my mind tells me he has no choice, but my heart doesn't understand that kind of logic."

Yesterday's Dream

"But what about us, David? You led me to think there was a chance for us." Some of the anger had left her tone, to be replaced by hurt.

"I suppose I was trying to convince myself of that, more so than to deceive you." He placed a hand on her shoulder and smiled contritely. "We're not of like mind, Becki. We're as well matched as Mom and Dad, and I saw first-hand how devastating that was. I wouldn't want to put my children through that."

She jerked her shoulder free. "I don't want kids."

His responding chuckle was humorless. "See what I mean?"

"I want to make music with you, Davie. I want us to hit it big someday in Branson or Nashville."

"I don't. I want a family and I want to teach. I have part of my dream now; perhaps someday, I'll have the other half."

"But not with Abigail," she reminded him with a taunting smirk.

"No, not with Abigail. And I'm still coming to terms with that."

"You're a fool, David."

"Not nearly as big a one if I pursued this further."

She tilted her chin defiantly and went on as though he hadn't rejected her. "We have the talent, Davie. All we need now is a break, and I bet if we hang in there, we'll eventually get that too."

He looked at her in disbelief mingled with pity. "Rebecca, you aren't listening. I don't want a career in music and . . . I really don't know how to say this delicately other than to come right out and say it. I don't want you either. I'm sorry, but you force me to be blunt, painfully so. Goodbye, Rebecca."

Becki opened her mouth to retort but she couldn't think of any thing cutting enough to say, so she slapped his cheek

160 *JoAnn Sands*

hard, then left, banging the door so viciously it made the window rattle.

The moment she was out of the house, Tricia hesitantly stuck her head in David's room. "You okay?"

"Yeah." His smile was an embarrassed one as his fingers massaged his stinging cheek. When his hand dropped to his side, her imprint was clearly visible.

Tricia gasped. "David! She hit you?"

His shrug was a dismissing one. "My words probably hurt her more than her slap hurt me. Anyway, I'm thankful I regained my sanity before I did something really stupid."

"Spending Saturday night with her was stupid, believe me."

"Nothing happened, Tricia. I watched her perform and, like the last time, she encouraged me to sing a couple of songs with her. The audience seemed to love it. Afterward, we went back to her place."

"And then?" she asked in dread.

"And then, nothing. I'm not used to drinking, and I passed out. I woke up the next morning, sick as a dog. It wasn't until one that I felt better, and I arrived home to face a very hurt and disappointed father. He jumped to all the wrong conclusions, and I was feeling too wretched inside to defend myself. I'm going to have to make it right with him. I never could sleep well when I'm on the outs with Dad."

"Me too. I knew I'd hurt him going to live with Sheila, trying to find myself." She smiled sadly. "Whatever that means."

"Did you? Find yourself, I mean."

"Yes. I found this is where I belong. My search is over —Laurel Springs is home."

He nodded, understanding exactly how she felt. He eyed her peach outfit. "I'll run you over to the Kenans, but I'm not going inside. I need time to reconcile the fact Abbie's

Yesterday's Dream 161

going to be another man's wife. Crazy as it sounds, I even toyed with the idea that Abbie and I could be Kevin's foster parents and give him a stable homelife. He could be in school with us. It would be perfect.''

"Daddy told me he wants to go to Brazil with Jamie.''

David grunted. "I suppose living in the jungle with caymans and anacondas sounds a whole lot more exciting to an eight-year-old than residing in a pastoral North Carolina community. But I must admit, I don't like that life-style for Abbie.''

"The way I hear, it'll only be for a year, then he's going to open a practice in the Kenan residence. However are you going to deal with that, David?''

"One day at a time, Tricia. One day at a time.''

A few minutes later, Tricia went out to the kitchen to make tuna salad sandwiches. She'd told David she wasn't going to the wedding either; she couldn't betray him like that. She was sure their father would understand and respect their decision. He wouldn't be there either, if he had a choice. He would smile and be cordial, she knew, but inside he would be hurting for his son. The Kenan women, she thought, had a way of unintentionally hurting the Rossi men. As she put coffee in the coffee machine, she could hear the rumble of distant thunder.

Tricia felt uneasy and spoke her thoughts as David entered the room, still shoeless. "I'm afraid Becki's right; we are gonna have a bad storm.''

When he saw the troubled expression on her face, he was reminded anew that she never outgrew her fear of spring and summer storms. "It's going to be all right, Patti,'' he said, reverting back to her former childhood name, for her demeanor had become childlike as those pesky old fears rose to catch her in their grip. "Nothing

JoAnn Sands

bad is going to happen,'' he further assured her, reaching out to give her hand a gentle squeeze. ''I won't let it.''

That boastful statement brought a nervous giggle from her lips, but only for a moment, for in the next second, the lights flickered then went out. ''Oh, no!'' she gasped. ''Something bad is going to happen.''

''Yep. It's going to rain on Jungle Jim's wedding,'' he said with a wicked grin. ''Pity, isn't it.''

Tricia laughed nervously—she couldn't help it—then caught herself. ''David, you're nasty.''

''I know,'' he winked. ''I'll get the candles just in case the power is off after dark. Unplug the radio and bring it over to the table, then switch it to battery operation. I put fresh ones in last week,'' he said, going to the closet.

Another clap of thunder, this one much louder, vibrated the windows. ''Oh, David, I'm really getting scared.''

''If you feel better, we could go down into the basement,'' he suggested, placing the candle on the table.

''The basement? You don't think we're actually going to have a . . .'' she broke off, unable to form the word.

David struck the match and placed it against the wick. The flame appeared, steady and bright. ''No, I don't think so.'' He shook the match out, glancing up at her. She carried the sandwiches, thick with tuna salad and lettuce, and sat them on their apple-shaped place mats. He went for the coffee and poured the beverage into their personalized mugs before setting down.

''I'll say grace,'' Tricia offered, but to him, it sounded more like a prayer for protection than a blessing on the food.

A few moments later, she draped her napkin over her skirt. ''I added a little relish to the tuna. Hope you like it that way.''

David bit into it, then smiled. ''Delicious! You've come a long way in such a short time, Tricia.''

Yesterday's Dream

"Thanks." She wiped a little squirt of mayonnaise from the corner of her mouth and mused for a moment. "I often wonder what would have become of me if it hadn't been for you and Daddy. Funny, but I could never think of Sheila as Mom."

"You're real mother died when you were ten and your biological father passed away when you were just a baby. So it's natural the way you've related to your new family." He smiled ruefully. "And don't feel guilty. It's hard for anyone to relate to Sheila as Mother. Take it from one who knows."

"I guess she hurt you too, huh."

David didn't answer; he didn't have to. She already knew. She took a sip of coffee, conscious of the howling wind. "It's picking up. What a night for a wedding! I wonder if the lights went out in the Kenan home."

"Wouldn't matter as I understand it's to be a candlelight service anyway. Romantic," he finished with a barb of bitterness.

"Oh David, I'm sorry. It doesn't seem to matter what I say, we keep circling back to the subject of Abbie."

"She's probably having the time of her life and isn't even aware of the weather." He looked across the table and smiled. "Thank you for spending the evening with me. It means a lot, you being here when I know you would have liked to have gone."

"Only if the groom were you," she said with feeling.

David felt an unexpected tearing at his eyes and a sudden lump. He tried to cover it by clearing his throat and shifting his thoughts to something else. Anything else but Abbie . . . she must be a vision in white. He practically made a dive for the radio and pressed the button for weather information.

". . . severe thunderstorms," the meteorologist was saying, "which could possibly spawn tornadoes."

164   *JoAnn Sands*

Tricia gasped, placing her mug down with a thump.

David placed a silencing finger to his lips. "Listen," he whispered, his eyes on the radio.

The conditions are right to put us under a watch. If we give you a warning that a tornado has been spotted, go into your basement. If you do not have a basement, choose a room with the fewest windows. Cover yourselves with a blanket and pillow to prevent getting cut from flying glass. If you're in a mobile home or a car, get out and take shelter at a friend's house or a public building. Keep tuned for further updates. And now, back to more music.

"Tornadoes," Tricia whispered once again, her face white from fear.

"Tornado watch," David corrected. "Patti, if you'd rather, we can go downstairs and wait it out."

"The building will fall in on us, just as it did the night Mama and Grandma died."

The look on her face drove all thoughts of pity for himself from his mind. He didn't want to have to deal with her blind panic on top of everything else. Elbows on the table, he leaned closer to her. "Tricia, listen to me. There's no reason to overreact. We're not in a trailer or car, we're in a house with a basement. Now, take a few deep breaths and finish your sandwich and coffee."

Nodding, she did as told, but David noticed her hands were shaking badly, and once again his heart went out to her, only imagining the terror she'd lived through once and was afraid of repeating again. A moment later his attention shifted to the radio, and he listened to the meteorologist who'd just broke into the regular programming. "Five funnel clouds have been spotted two miles southeast of Laurel

Yesterday's Dream 165

Springs and are heading toward that community. I repeat . . .''

David pushed his chair back and rose. ''It might be a good idea to go to the basement now.'' He reached for her hand, but her fear had turned to panic.

''We're going to die!'' she screamed as she ran into the living room, stumbling over the umbrella Becki had thrown down.

''Patti!'' David shouted, ''Don't go out there!''

But she was beyond reasoning. The teen yanked the door open and ran blindly into the storm and into the path of danger!

Chapter Twelve

"Here's the something borrowed, Abbie," Ruby said, handing her a single string of real pearls. "My sister inherited these from the lady she took care of for years, and they were given to me when my sister passed on."

"Thanks, Rube. I'll take real good care of them," she promised, stooping a little so the housekeeper could easily fasten the clasp around her neck.

"If only your daddy could see you now, he'd be mighty proud of his little girl. You sure do your mama's gown justice."

Abbie stared at her image in the full-length mirror. She did look radiant, this was true, yet there was something lacking, something she couldn't quite put her finger on— or could she?

Ruby stood behind her, viewing her image. She noted the puckered brow, the restless fingers worrying her necklace. "Cold feet?"

Abbie's hand slid to her side and she turned to face Ruby. "Not cold feet, just the bridal-day jitters, I guess. You know how it is."

"I sure do, honey," she agreed with a shoulder-shaking

166

chuckle. "It was the most excitin' day of my life when I took Ukee as my husband. What a fine-lookin' man he was, all decked out in his good black suit. Kind of like he looks today, real handsome."

"So are you," Abbie said, admiring her new silk lilac dress. On it she had pinned a showy corsage. Ruby noticed her gaze and responded proudly as she touched it. "Magnolia blossoms. It was Jamie's idea. Said they stand for dignity and he couldn't think of a more befittin' flower for ol' Ruby."

"Nor can I." Abbie's smile was a pensive one, then she changed the subject. "I had a dream last night, about the wedding."

"Oh? What'd you do, faint dead away at the altar?"

Now Abbie laughed. "No, nothing like that. You know the part where the preacher says to the congregation about speaking up now or forever hold your peace? Well, David came bursting into the parlor and said his father had no right to be marrying us because he loved me."

"What happened then?" she asked when Abbie's voice trailed off and she stared unblinking at an area of the floor. She pulled her eyes away and up to Ruby's kind, caring face, then shrugged. "I woke up."

"How did it make you feel about David, bustin' in on your weddin' like that?"

"Anger and relief. I'm not quite sure which emotion was the strongest. Does it matter? Such an outburst only ever happens in the movies and old novels."

"Dreams can sometimes bring out thoughts our consciousness has suppressed."

"Why Ruby Brown," Abbie said, trying to sound more carefree than she actually felt. "You been hitting Daddy's old psychology books?"

"Just an observer of people."

"I love him."

"Which one?"

"If you need to ask . . ." Abbie broke off, her patience slipping.

"You need to answer," Ruby said boldly. "It's still not too late, you know."

"Not too late?" she echoed. "Ruby, our guests are congregating in the parlor this very minute."

"They would understand."

"Not Mother. Jamie's her ideal. Kind, thoughtful Jamie is every mother's ideal."

A lump caught in Abbie's throat as the woman who'd been her nanny placed her arms around her and held her just as she did when she was a little girl. There was comfort now, as there had been then. "I love him, Ruby," she whispered through her tears of confusion. "I do love him."

"Who, honey? Who do you love?"

Abigail drew back and looked her defiantly in the eye. "Jamie."

Jamie felt stiff and out of place in his tuxedo. He'd never had an occasion to wear one before in his thirty-three years, but he would now to make Abbie and her mother happy. Nervous, he began to wander around the well-equipped office, marveling that Maggie still kept it in a state of readiness for someone to move right in and take over. And it looked as though he, Jamie MacIlhaney, would be the one. This was, as Maggie had said repeatedly, the chance of a lifetime. That very morning, he had visited the small local hospital to familiarize himself with the place he would be affiliated with. He met the heads of cardiology and pediatrics. It was so well equipped. Had he only been privy to such technology in his jungle clinic, he could have saved many more lives. He thought of some of his recent patients and a smile played on his lips. He was still musing when Kevin walked in a few minutes later.

Yesterday's Dream

Jamie turned and looked at the boy, his smile spreading even deeper across his thin face. "Just look at ye lad. You're a handsome sight, ye are," he exclaimed, exaggerating his accent.

Kevin rubbed at his scratchy, stiff collar. "If this is what it takes to be handsome, I'd rather be scuffy. At least that's comfortable."

Jamie tossed back his head and laughed. "I know what you mean, but I suppose we can put up with it for a few hours if it makes the womenfolk happy."

"I suppose so," he reluctantly agreed, then studied the man a moment before going on. "Now that you and Abbie are married, or will be in minutes, do you think maybe you could adopt me? I'll be good, I promise. Maggie says I'm improving."

"I'm sure you are."

"Well, can I?" he pressed. "I mean, may I," Kevin corrected, remembering how Abbie was after him to use proper English. "I'll be able to help you in the jungle. I ain't afraid of no bugs nor spiders either, no matter how big," he boasted, slipping back into his usual speech pattern. "So, what do you think?"

A knock on the door interrupted Jamie from telling him just what he thought. Maggie opened the door wide enough to stick her head inside. "Bill's arrived. It's time we begin."

At that point, lightning flashed, followed by a loud clap of thunder, and then the lights went out. But Maggie hardly skipped a beat. "Never mind," she said, in the dimness bordering on darkness made worse by the thick clouds. "The candles are lit the parlor. It will all add to the memory of the evening. Kevin, honey, give me your hand and we'll walk down the stairs together."

After seeing them safely to the entrance of the parlor, Maggie retrieved a flashlight and went back for Abbie. She was now alone, standing at the window, looking out at the storm.

"No, this isn't exactly how I envisioned my daughter's wedding day," the woman said, knowing Abbie's thoughts. "But it's out of our hands. I only hope everyone's here that intends to come."

Abbie turned, her face etched with anxiety. "I'm worried, Mom. This doesn't seem to be an ordinary storm. The sky's so strange looking."

Without further conversation, Abbie joined her mother and they made their way down the stairs. Lucille's lovely soprano voice could be heard singing "Oh Love, Thou Wilt Not Let Me Go," a favorite of Jamie's, while she accompanied herself on the baby grand.

They stopped before the double parlor doors and watched the small gathering. Lucille's voice grew louder on the second stanza, not to be drowned out by the noise outside. It sounded like a freight train. Abbie looked at her mother and noticed a slight tightening of her jaw muscles, but if she was frightened, her voice didn't betray her as she patted Abbie's cold hands and whispered, "Everything's going to be all right, honey. We're safe inside these thick old walls. Besides, it's rare that a tornado would hit this part of the state."

Tornado! Abbie thought wildly, her eyes turning to Lucille, who'd stopped singing altogether now, waiting until that dreadful sound which literally rattled the windows stopped.

Realizing she'd been holding her breath in fear, Abbie exhaled and watched as Bill and Jamie walked to the portable altar in front of the dozen guests. Seeing this khaki-wearing jungle doctor all dressed up brought a smile to her lips, and she momentarily put the storm from her mind. What a gorgeous sight he was in his rented black tuxedo and white ruffled shirt. His brown hair was shining and

Yesterday's Dream

wavy, just barely touching his collar. He reminded her of a classical musician on opening night—the attire, the nervousness he tried to hide behind a smile, the wrinkled brow. Subconsciously, he cracked his knuckles and flexed his long fingers.

Are you having second thoughts, Jamie? she wondered. Or does this gathering, small though it is, intimidate you? Then her gaze shifted to Kevin. He was too young to be the best man yet too old to be the ring bearer that he was.

Abbie searched the guests for David and Tricia, but they were conspicuously missing. Just as well, she thought, for when Bill got to the part where he said, ''speak now or forever hold your peace,'' last night's dream might become a reality. David was not going to rescue her.

Rescue her? The very thought sent a shock wave through her body. She loved Jamie, and in a few minutes, he would take her as his wife, by the powers invested in William Rossi.

Lucille began to play once again. This was the cue for mother and daughter to walk down the aisle together, and for Maggie to have the honor of giving her to Jamie. But before they could enter the parlor, a man whom Abbie recognized from the congregation came up behind them. He was clearly upset.

''Abigail,'' he whispered breathlessly. ''Forgive me, but I must speak to Bill.''

''Really, Tom,'' Maggie spoke up before Abbie could. ''Can't it wait? There's a wedding going on.''

Abbie laid her hand on the distressed man's arm. ''Go on. We're not at the altar yet.''

Margaret turned indignantly to her daughter the moment the man slipped through the door. ''You shouldn't have done that, Abigail,'' she chided. ''It isn't proper.''

The bride shook her head. ''Something awful must have happened or he wouldn't even consider seeing Bill at such a time as this.'' Her eyes stayed on the man, who stood dripping raindrops on the white runner as he spoke to Bill in an excited whisper. Curious, Jamie joined the pair and they spoke in subdued tones. Abbie saw Jamie nod, then Bill stepped forward and began to speak urgently.

"I'm sorry to have to do this after we've all gathered together, but the ceremony must be postponed till later this evening. If not this evening, then tomorrow at this time."

Abbie gasped. Maggie drew her arm around her daughter and listened as Bill continued. "Thomas has just informed me that a tornado has struck my property and did some damage to my house. He went inside but couldn't find my children. I must see that they're okay. As you're all aware, Patti's terrified of storms ever since her mother died in one. If they're all right, we'll meet back here and proceed with the ceremony."

The men in attendance rose and offered to help. Bill gratefully accepted their offers, then walked to the doorway and took Abbie's hands in his. "Forgive me for doing this to you, Abigail, but I must know if . . ." his voice trailed off, unable to form the words.

Abbie gave him a gentle, comforting squeeze. "I understand. I'll be praying that you find them safe and unharmed."

Jamie came up behind him. "Abigail, would you mind very much if I went along?"

If they're hurt, he could help, she thought, but didn't say this out loud. Instead she braved a smile. "I think that would be a good idea. I'll come with you."

"Abigail," Maggie chided once again. "Don't you think it would be wiser if you waited with the rest of the women in the parlor where it's warm and dry? Hopefully, we can continue this in the next hour."

"I can't, Mom. I can't sit. I'd pace the floor, wondering what happened to . . . to Bill's children."

Yesterday's Dream

"I suppose you know what's best for you," Maggie relented. Nonetheless, she looked distressed at the idea. Yet, in another moment, she too had made up her mind. "Perhaps I'd better join you. Jamie might need some help if the unthinkable has happened." Turning to Ruby, she instructed her to stay with the guests and for Ukee to keep an eye on Kevin, who was balking about being left behind.

Abbie slipped into more comfortable shoes while Jamie went for his medical bag and they left, a caravan of six automobiles, speeding to the Rossi home, fearful of what they might find.

It was standing, though the yard was littered with uprooted trees. One had fallen across the front porch, collapsing the roof and breaking a window. The door stood open at a strange angle, blown off one of its hinges.

"David!" Abbie called, shining her flashlight through the open door. "Are you inside?"

No reply.

"Tricia!" she shouted, her voice joining the others who were searching the yard, casting their beams back and forth, pushing back the darkness, while an excited Shadow ran around in wild circles, barking. Abbie looked up miserably at Jamie. "We've got to find them."

"And we will, Abigail. Careful where you walk or you'll soil your gown. You look mighty pretty," he complimented with a melancholy smile. "I think they say it's bad luck for the groom to see his bride before the wedding."

"I'm so sorry, Jamie. I didn't mean to ruin your wedding day." Mindful, she held her dress up to her calves and shone the light around with her free hand, while Jamie held the large black umbrella over their heads. Her worst fear had been David disrupting her wedding, though disrupting it in this manner never crossed her mind. But she didn't care that it was disrupted, so long as he was safe.

She walked slowly forward, sticks and twigs snapping under her sneakers. The flashlight beam caught a glimmer of gold embedded in the dirt. Stooping, she gingerly worked it loose and lifted it up to the light.

"What is it?"

"Tricia's necklace. It was a birthday gift from her father years ago. She always wears it. She's got to be around here."

"Tricia!" she called out, walking away from the house to the path the tornado had taken. Shadow was a short distance away, barking excitedly and scratching at the soil. Then she saw it. A bare arm—David's arm—just visible under the branches of the uprooted pine. "Oh no!"

"Wait!" Jamie cautioned, catching her by the elbow as she went to make a dive for him. "I'll look. You hold the beam steady."

Abbie obeyed his command, sending up a frantic prayer as Jamie's fingers closed over David's wrist in an effort to find a pulse. "He's alive," he said, without looking back at her. Then, "There appears to be someone lying beneath him."

"It must be Tricia."

Now Jamie looked over at the men combing the debris-littered yard with their own flashlights. "We've found them!" he called. "Can anyone get their hands on a chain-saw to get them free?"

Twenty minutes later, the tree was cut into sections and carried away to expose the brother who had covered his sister's body with his own to protect her. Abbie watched in hope and despair as their limp bodies were gently laid side by side on the wet grass. Bill stood over them, grim-faced, as he held the light. "How bad is it?"

"I can't be sure yet. If anyone has a cell phone in their car, call for an ambulance. Maggie, I could use a bit of

Yesterday's Dream 175

your help. It appears David has a concussion, and Tricia's lung has collapsed.'' He began cutting away at the girl's silky shirt. ''Get a McSwain Dart and scalpel from my bag and assist me,'' he ordered, his hands occupied. He didn't like it. Tricia's skin was a frightening shade of blue.

''What can I do, Jamie?'' Abbie asked.

''Just keep your hand steady as you give me light,'' he said, making a small incision between her ribs. ''And pray for these two that we won't lose them.''

Bill sat in the small waiting room of the hospital, scarcely aware that he'd been clasping Maggie's hand. ''I can't lose my kids,'' he mumbled again. ''We were finally beginning to heal and be a family again. I feel as though I've failed them. Tricia's always been terrified of storms. When one would come up, I'd take her into the basement and close the drapes so she wouldn't be quite as aware of the lightning and the wind.''

''Bill, you must stop blaming yourself,'' Maggie said gently, stroking the hand that was gripping hers. ''It wasn't your fault. It wasn't anyone's fault—it just happened.''

''But why?'' He turned to face her, his expression creased with hurt and worry. ''Why do these things happen? You know, I counsel people in crisis situations all the time, but it just occurred to me I never really understood how helpless they felt until now.''

''I believe there are reasons, Bill. Sometimes they are made known, sometimes they're not. Hopefully some good will come out of a bad situation. But I do know this. You mustn't lose your faith, Bill. You must be strong, no matter what the outcome. And don't tell me I don't know what I'm talking about. I've lost two of the people closest to me. I didn't give up, and neither must you.''

Bill braved a smile, his free hand coming down on top of hers. ''I'm glad you and Abbie offered to stay with me,

176   *JoAnn Sands*

but I've intruded horribly on your time—on your special day, your wedding day, Abigail," he said, turning to the girl who sat stiffly beside him. "I'll make it up to you and Jamie somehow, I promise."

She nodded mutely and stared at the hem of her mud-splattered gown. Jamie, she thought with a deep sigh. Regardless of which way it went with David, she couldn't go through with their marriage. It simply wouldn't be fair to Jamie. He deserved better. He deserved someone who could love him totally and not be encumbered with such deep feeling for another.

Abbie looked up at the sound of footsteps. Jamie had entered the room. He looked haggard, his soiled white shirt bearing testimony of an affair going horribly wrong. There was no smile on his face, only weariness and defeat.

"Oh no," Bill groaned, slumping back.

Jamie was quick to shake his head, knowing his thoughts and wanting to cut his agony short. "They're both out of danger and expected to make a full recovery. Tricia's arm is fractured and David sustained a moderate concussion, but he's awake now."

"Thank heaven," Bill said with a catch in his throat. "And . . . and thank you, Jamie. I owe you a debt of gratitude I can never repay."

Abbie's eyes remained fixed on his. All was not right. She spoke her thoughts. "Then why do you look so sad, Jamie? I've only ever seen that expression on your face after you've fought hard to save a patient, but couldn't."

"We have to talk, Abigail, in private."

"There's nothing you can't say in front of my mother and Bill. So, what is it?"

"You have to ask?" He sat down on the empty chair beside her. "Abigail, you never told me about David. I had to learn of him when he walked in on us at the school."

Yesterday's Dream

"We've been through this before. I explained to you we were old friends."

"Yes. And you led me to believe there were no feelings between you. But there are, Abigail, there are very deep feelings as far as David's concerned, and I don't know what to do with that."

"Jamie . . ." She broke off, drawing in a stabilizing breath. How she dreaded doing this to such a kind man. "Jamie, I was going to marry you tonight, and had that storm not struck when it did, we would be man and wife now."

"Yes, and that would be wrong. No," he said, when she opened her mouth to try and let him down easily. "Let me finish. Your parents' wish always was for you to marry a physician, just like your father. By the time I came along, your relationship with David had cooled to a warm cozy memory. But Abigail, I am not Jeremy Kenan. Your mother has offered me a golden opportunity . . . my own practice in a town whose closest physician is twenty miles away. I'm sure there are those who would tell me I'm crazy, but my heart is not in Laurel Springs. It is the jungles of Brazil, where the nearest doctor is five hundred miles away. They need me, and it's my calling to be there for them. A famous martyr once said, 'He is no fool who gives what he cannot keep to gain what he cannot lose.' Profound words they were, from a young man killed by the very natives he was trying to teach."

Jamie paused and swallowed. It was a difficult speech to make but it had to be said. "I love you, Abigail, but I love my calling more. I believe it's possible to love two things at once, just as I feel it's possible for you to love two totally different men at once. In the end, though, I sense your love for David is deeper. I saw your tears. They were rolling down your cheeks the entire time I was working on him. And when he woke up a short time ago, it was your name

178 *JoAnn Sands*

he was saying over and over. In spite of your years of separation, your love hasn't died. It was only submerged— and now it's rising to the surface, stronger than ever. We came very close to exchanging vows this evening. I think David will agree that a concussion was a small price to pay to stop the wedding he couldn't bear to witness.''

''Oh, Jamie, everything you're saying is true,'' she admitted with a little sob. ''And . . . and I'm so sorry.''

''I know, but then,'' he said with a worn smile, ''God works in mysterious ways sometimes. You'd better go to David now, Abbie,'' he finished, a tear rolling down his cheek.

Abigail made a strange spectacle as she ran through the hospital corridor in her maddy wedding gown, but she was too intent on her mission to notice the curious stares of the visitors and staff. Now at David's bedside, she stood breathless and studied his branch-scraped face. ''David?'' she whispered, unsure.

His eyes flickered open, then closed. ''I must be dreaming.''

''No you're not. It's me, Abbie, in the flesh,'' she assured him as she took his hand in hers and brought it to her mouth to kiss it. ''I'm so sorry you were hurt.''

He gasped, his eyes flashing open once again as her words jarred him awake and memory returned. ''Tricia!''

''Her arm's broken, but she's going to be okay. You both are.'' She smiled through misty eyes. ''You're a hero, David. You saved your sister's life at the risk of losing your own. Sometimes it takes something pretty drastic to get our attention, to get us back on track.''

''I don't know what you're talking about.'' He stared at her for a moment. ''Shouldn't you be off on your honeymoon with Crocodile Dundee about now?''

Yesterday's Dream 179

She shook her head, not chiding him for that disparaging remark. "Jamie sent me to you."

"Magnanimous of him."

"You say that with sarcasm, but consider that he donated a pint of his own blood to give you back the one you lost."

"Oh, great! Now can I expect to suddenly get the urge to wrestle alligators or gorillas?"

Abbie shook her head hopelessly, not remembering him to be so contrary, but then that was his way of coping. "David, don't be so obstinate. It doesn't become you."

He stared up at her glumly. "You don't have to be my nurse maid, Abbie. This isn't right. You should be with your hus . . . husband." The word stuck in his throat and he wanted to gag on it.

"What husband?"

"Abigail, please. My head's throbbing, and I'm in no mood for games."

"The wedding's off."

David blinked up at her, wanting to believe, yet not able to. "Yeah, for now."

"Forever."

"Really?" A slow comprehending smile spread across his face. Then, thinking better of his reaction, he changed his expression. "Gee, I'm sorry to hear that, Ab."

"No you're not."

"All right, I'm not. Right or wrong, I've never stopped loving you, Abbie. Even when I thought I'd lost you."

"I know, darling. I've never stopped loving you either. I want you to close your eyes now and go to sleep."

"I can't. If I do that, I'm afraid when I wake up, I'll find this conversation never happened—that it was all a dream due to the medication."

"No you won't. When you wake up, you will find me here beside you. I promise," she said, sealing it with a kiss.

* * *

180   *JoAnn Sands*

Abbie didn't return home until daybreak, after David had awakened and seen that she'd kept her promise. When she left, he was in better spirits.

After showering and changing into jeans and a tee shirt, she entered the kitchen to find her mother waiting for her, sipping her morning coffee. There was a fresh arrangement of flowers sitting on the table. Abbie froze in her tracks, staring at it.

"Well, aren't you going to open the card?" Maggie gently prodded.

"I don't have to. They're from Jamie. The Michaelmas daisy means 'farewell.' He took a jar of them to Delores' gravesite once when I was with him. I don't know which is harder on him—losing her or me." Abbie pulled out a chair and sat down. Her mood swings had been uncharacteristically up and down all night—now they were plummeting. "Oh, Mom, I'm so sorry about all this."

"No, it's I who's sorry. I pushed you into it. I was living my life vicariously through you, Abbie. Your father and I were so happy, but it's as Jamie said last night, he's not Jeremy. And you're no Maragret, I might add. You're you, and you must do what's best for Abigail Kenan. So, having said that, can you forgive me?"

Abbie nodded as she touched one of the petals. She blinked tears back. "When did he leave?"

"Last night, as soon as he came back from the hospital. Bill and I drove him to the airport. We talked it over, and we think the congregation will want to get the money together to send your father's equipment to Brazil. I can't think of a better use of it, can you?"

"No, I can't." She braved a smile, and wiped a stray tear from her cheek. "He was like a little boy on Christmas morning when I gave him Daddy's medical bag. Good thing I did too, for he used the McSwain Dart to save Tri-

Yesterday's Dream

cia. Someday, we'll read great things about Jamie's work in South America.''

''I'm sure we will, honey. He's found his niche in life, just as you and David have.''

In another moment, Abbie was hugging her mother. The hurt was still fresh. One moment she was laughing over David, the next weeping for Jamie. She had been struggling to find the words in the waiting room to cancel the wedding, while he, having come to the same conclusion, spared her the agony by doing it for her. It was for the best, and soon she would know in her heart what her head already knew.

Epilogue

Two days later, Abbie drove David and Tricia home from the hospital. David sat beside her, unusually quiet and Abbie finally asked him what was on his mind.

"Our parents. Is there something going on between them I'm not aware of?"

"Oh, I think you're aware or you wouldn't be asking. I'm not sure what the catalyst was—the tornado or Kevin—but the three of them have become inseparable. She wants to keep Kevin now as much as he wants to stay. Motherhood's a natural for Mom. We're going to talk to Ms. Wells's supervisor and get her to see Mom could provide the perfect environment for him."

Tricis sat tranquilly in the back seat. As they passed the church, hope swelled within her that she would see that desired welcoming banner, but there wasn't any. You don't really need a sign, she told herself. You know Daddy loves you by his actions. He just has a hard time expressing it in so many words.

They drove a couple of blocks in silence, each occupied with his or her own thoughts. Abbie pulled up alongside the curb and turned the ignition off. David straightened up,

Yesterday's Dream 183

surprised. Members of the congregation were sawing up the blown down trees and stacking them in the corner of the property. The yard was a buzz of activity. Ukee was supervising the men who were dismantling the front porch, destroyed by the fallen pine tree. But Tricia's attention was focused on the wind-rippled banner in front of the house for the entire community to see. Between its two wooden posts were painted the words WELCOME HOME, TRICIA AND DAVID.

Tricia looked at Abbie, tears misting her vision. Abbie nodded, knowing her thoughts, but before either could speak, the door was opened by Bill Rossi and he extended his hand to her.

"Welcome home, Tricia," he stated with feeling.

A tide of warmth and acceptance washed over her, and it felt soooo good. "Thanks, Daddy, but you may call me Patti now."

He looked perplexed, but Margaret did not. Patricia didn't need to question her identity any more. She was quite comfortable with who she was. He continued, "You arrived at just the right time, honey. We're about ready to break for lunch. A group of ladies from the auxiliary made bean soup and beef barbecue."

"And there's Ruby's peach pie and ice cream for dessert!" Kevin exclaimed, running up behind Maggie. "She's some cook!"

The adults surrounding him broke into laughter, while Margaret gave the child a hug. "Wash your hands. We're ready to gather around the table and eat."

Abbie and David stood alone for a moment and watched the others walk away—Bill with his arm around Patti's shoulder and Kevin with his hand securely tucked in Maggie's. Abbie too felt happy and secure as she sought David's hand. He gave it a light squeeze, knowing they were facing life together. Not as a couple of star-struck teens, but as partners in education, turning the lives of future Kevins and Tricias into something good and productive. It had been worth the wait—for all of them.